"I should go."

Ana set her glass down before it could slip out of her trembling hand. "I really only meant to stay a minute."

"Ana." Boone shifted, blocking the way in case she sprinted for the door. "I have a feeling what just happened here was out of character for both of us. That's interesting, don't you think?"

She lifted those solemn gray eyes to his. "I don't know your character."

"Well, I don't make a habit of seducing women in the kitchen when my daughter's upstairs. And I certainly don't make a habit out of wanting the hell out of a woman the minute I lay eyes on her."

"I suppose you want me to say I'll take your word for it. But I won't."

Both anger and challenge sparked in his eyes. "Then I'll have to prove it to you, won't I?"

Dear Reader:

Romance readers have been enthusiastic about the Silhouette Special Editions for years. And that's not by accident: Special Editions were the first of their kind and continue to feature realistic stories with heightened romantic tension.

The longer stories, sophisticated style, greater sensual detail and variety that made Special Editions popular are the same elements that will make you want to read book after book.

We hope that you enjoy this Special Edition today, and will enjoy many more.

Please write to us:

Jane Nicholls
Silhouette Books
PO Box 236
Thornton Road
Croydon
Surrey
CR9 3RU

NORA ROBERTS
Charmed

Silhouette Special Edition

Originally Published by Silhouette Books
a division of
Harlequin Enterprises Ltd.

*First published in Great Britain in 1993
by Silhouette Books, Eton House, 18-24 Paradise Road,
Richmond, Surrey TW9 1SR*

© Nora Roberts 1992

*Silhouette, Silhouette Special Edition and Colophon are
Trade Marks of Harlequin Enterprises B.V.*

ISBN 0 373 58760 0

23-9303

Made and printed in Great Britain

To everyone who believes in happy endings.

Other Silhouette Books by Nora Roberts

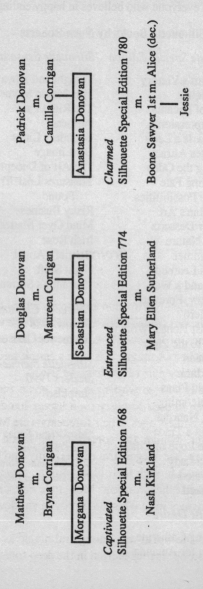

Matthew Donovan
m.
Bryna Corrigan

Morgana Donovan

Captivated
Silhouette Special Edition 768
m.
Nash Kirkland

Douglas Donovan
m.
Maureen Corrigan

Sebastian Donovan

Entranced
Silhouette Special Edition 774
m.
Mary Ellen Sutherland

Padrick Donovan
m.
Camilla Corrigan

Anastasia Donovan

Charmed
Silhouette Special Edition 780
m.
Boone Sawyer 1st m. Alice (dec.)

Jessie

Prologue

Magic exists. Who can doubt it, when there are rainbows and wildflowers, the music of the wind and the silence of the stars? Anyone who has loved has been touched by magic. It is such a simple and such an extraordinary part of the lives we live.

There are those who have been given more, who have been chosen to carry on a legacy handed down through endless ages. Their forebears were Merlin the enchanter, Ninian the sorceress, the faerie princess Rhiannon, the Wegewarte of Germany and the jinns of Arabia. Through their blood ran the power of Finn of the Celts, the ambitious Morgan le Fay, and others whose names were whispered only in shadows and in secret.

When the world was young and magic as common as a raindrop, faeries danced in the deep forests, and—

sometimes for mischief, sometimes for love—mixed with mortals.

And they do still.

Her bloodline was old. Her power was ancient. Even as a child she had understood, had been taught, that such gifts were not without price. The loving parents who treasured her could not lower the cost, or pay it themselves, but could only love, instruct and watch the young girl grow to womanhood. They could only stand and hope as she experienced the pains and the joys of that most fascinating of journeys.

And, because she felt more than others, because her gift demanded that she feel more, she learned to court peace.

As a woman, she preferred a quiet life, and was often alone without the pain of loneliness.

As a witch, she accepted her gift, and never forgot the responsibility it entailed.

Perhaps she yearned, as mortals and others have yearned since the beginning, for a true and abiding love. For she knew better than most that there was no power, no enchantment, no sorcery, greater than the gift of an open and accepting heart.

Chapter One

When she saw the little girl peek through the fairy roses, Anastasia had no idea the child would change her life. She'd been humming to herself, as she often did when she gardened, enjoying the scent and the feel of earth. The warm September sun was golden, and the gentle whoosh of the sea on the rocks below her sloping yard was a lovely background to the buzzing of bees and the piping of birdsong. Her long gray cat was stretched out beside her, his tail twitching in time with some feline dream.

A butterfly landed soundlessly on her hand, and she stroked the edge of its pale blue wings with a fingertip. As it fluttered off, she heard the rustling. Glancing over, she saw a small face peeping through the hedge of fairy roses.

Ana's smile came quickly, naturally. The face was charming, with its little pointed chin and its pert nose, its big blue eyes mirroring the color of the sky. A pixie cap of glossy brown hair completed the picture.

The girl smiled back, those summer-sky eyes full of curiosity and mischief.

"Hello," Ana said, as if she always found little girls in her rosebushes.

"Hi." The girl's voice was bright, and a little breathless. "Can you catch butterflies? I never got to pet one like that before."

"I suppose. But it seems rude to try unless one invites you." She brushed the hair from her brow with her forearm and sat back on her heels. Ana had noticed a moving van unloading the day before, and she concluded she was meeting one of her new neighbors. "Have you moved into the house next door?"

"Uh-huh. We're going to live here now. I like it, 'cause I get to look right out my bedroom window and see the water. I saw a seal, too. In Indiana you only see them in the zoo. Can I come over?"

"Of course you can." Ana set her garden spade aside as the girl stepped through the rosebushes. In her arms was a wriggling puppy. "And who do we have here?"

"This is Daisy." The child pressed a loving kiss to the top of the puppy's head. "She's a golden retriever. I got to pick her out myself right before we left Indiana. She got to fly in the plane with us, and we were hardly scared at all. I have to take good care of her and give her food and water and brush her and everything, 'cause she's my responsibility."

"She's very beautiful," Ana said soberly. And very heavy, she imagined, for a little girl of five or six. She held out her arms. "May I?"

"Do you like dogs?" The little girl kept chattering as she passed Daisy over. "I do. I like dogs and cats and everything. Even the hamsters Billy Walker has. Someday I'm going to have a horse, too. We'll have to see about that. That's what my daddy says. We'll have to see about that."

Utterly charmed, Ana stroked the puppy as she sniffed and licked at her. The child was as sweet as sunshine. "I'm very fond of dogs and cats and everything," Ana told her. "My cousin has horses. Two big ones and a brand-new baby."

"Really?" The child squatted down and began to pet the sleeping cat. "Can I see them?"

"He doesn't live far, so perhaps one day. We'll have to ask your parents."

"My mommy went to heaven. She's an angel now."

Ana's heart broke a little. Reaching out, she touched the shiny hair and opened herself. There was no pain here, and that was a relief. The memories were good ones. At the touch, the child looked up and smiled.

"I'm Jessica," she said. "But you can call me Jessie."

"I'm Anastasia." Because it was too much to resist, Ana bent down and kissed the pert nose. "But you can call me Ana."

Introductions over, Jessie settled down to bombard Ana with questions, filtering information about herself through the bright chatter. She'd just had a birthday and was six. She would be starting first grade in her brand-new school on Tuesday. Her favorite color was purple, and she hated lima beans more than anything.

Could Ana show her how to plant flowers? Did her cat have a name? Did she have any little girls? Why not?

So they sat in the sunshine, a bright pixie of a girl in pink rompers and a woman with garden dirt smearing her shorts and her lightly tanned legs, while Quigley the cat ignored the playful attentions of Daisy the dog.

Ana's long, wheat-colored hair was tied carelessly back, and the occasional wisp worked free of the band to dance in the wind around her face. She wore no cosmetics. Her fragile, heartbreaking beauty was as natural as her power, a combination of Celtic bones, smoky eyes, the wide, poetically sculptured Donovan mouth—and something more nebulous. Her face was the mirror of a giving heart.

The pup marched over to sniff at the herbs in her rockery. Ana laughed at something Jessica said.

"Jessie!" The voice swept over the hedge of roses, deeply male, and touched with exasperation and concern. "Jessica Alice Sawyer!"

"Uh-oh. He used my whole name." But Jessie's eyes were twinkling as she jumped to her feet. There was obviously little fear of reprisals.

"Over here! Daddy, I'm right over here with Ana! Come and see!"

A moment later, there was a man towering over the fairy roses. No gift was needed to detect waves of frustration, relief and annoyance. Ana blinked once, surprised that this rough-and-ready male was the father of the little sprite currently bouncing beside her.

Maybe it was the day or two's growth of beard that made him look so dangerous, she thought. But she doubted it. Beneath that dusky shadow was a sharp-featured face of planes and angles, a full mouth set in grim lines. Only the eyes were like his daughter's, a clear, brilliant blue, marred now by an expression of impatience. The sun brought out glints of red in his dark, tousled hair as he dragged a hand through it.

From her perch on the ground, he looked enormous. Athletically fit and disconcertingly strong, in a ripped T-shirt and faded jeans sprung at the seams.

He cast one long, annoyed and unmistakably distrustful glance at Ana before giving his attention to his daughter.

"Jessica. Didn't I tell you to stay in the yard?"

"I guess." She smiled winningly. "Daisy and I heard Ana singing, and when we looked, she had this butterfly right on her hand. And she said we could come over. She has a cat, see? And her cousin has horses, and her other cousin has a cat *and* a dog."

Obviously used to Jessie's rambling, her father waited it out. "When I tell you to stay in the yard, and then you're not there, I'm going to worry."

It was a simple statement, made in even tones. Ana had to respect the fact that the man didn't have to raise his voice or spout ultimatums to get his point across. She felt every bit as chastened as Jessie.

"I'm sorry, Daddy," Jessie murmured over a pouting lower lip.

"I should apologize, Mr. Sawyer." Ana rose to lay a hand on Jessie's shoulder. After all, it looked as if they were in this together. "I did invite her over, and I was enjoying her company so much that it didn't occur to me that you wouldn't be able to see where she was."

He said nothing for a moment, just stared at her with those water-clear eyes until she had to fight the urge to squirm. When he flicked his gaze down to his daughter again, Ana realized she'd been holding her breath.

"You should take Daisy over and feed her."

"Okay." Jessie hauled the reluctant pup into her arms, then stopped when her father inclined his head.

"And thank Mrs...?"

"Miss," Ana supplied. "Donovan. Anastasia Donovan."

"Thank Miss Donovan for putting up with you."

"Thank you for putting up with me, Ana," Jessie said with singsong politeness, sending Ana a conspirator's grin. "Can I come back?"

"I hope you will."

As she stepped through the bushes, Jessie offered her father a sunny smile. "I didn't mean to make you worry, Daddy. Honest."

He bent down and tweaked her nose. "Brat." Ana heard the wealth of love behind the exasperation.

With a giggle, Jessie ran across the yard, the puppy wriggling in her arms. Ana's smile faded the moment those cool blue eyes turned back to her.

"She's an absolutely delightful child," Ana began, amazed that she had to wipe damp palms on her shorts. "I do apologize for not making certain you knew where she was, but I hope you'll let her come back to visit me again."

"It wasn't your responsibility." His voice was cool, neither friendly nor unfriendly. Ana had the uncomfortable certainty that she was being weighed, from the top of her head to the bottom of her grass-stained sneakers. "Jessie is naturally curious and friendly. Sometimes too much of both. It doesn't occur to her that there are people in the world who might take advantage of that."

Equally cool now, Ana inclined her head. "Point taken, Mr. Sawyer. Though I can assure you I rarely gobble up young girls for breakfast."

He smiled, a slow curving of the lips that erased the harshness from his face and replaced it with a devastating appeal. "You certainly don't fit my perception of an ogre, Miss Donovan. Now I'll have to apologize for being so abrupt. She gave me a scare. I hadn't even unpacked yet, and I'd lost her."

"Misplaced." Ana tried another cautious smile. She looked beyond him to the two-story redwood house next door, with its wide band of windows and its curvy deck. Though she was content in her privacy, she was glad it hadn't remained empty long. "It's nice to have a child nearby, especially one as entertaining as Jessie. I hope you'll let her come back."

"I often wonder if I *let* her do anything." He flicked a finger over a tiny pink rose. "Unless you replace these with a ten-foot wall, she'll be back." And at least he'd know where to look if she disappeared again. "Don't be afraid to send her home when she overstays her welcome." He tucked his hands in his pockets. "I'd better go make sure she doesn't feed Daisy our dinner."

"Mr. Sawyer?" Ana said as he turned away. "Enjoy Monterey."

"Thanks." His long strides carried him over the lawn, onto the deck and into the house.

Ana stood where she was for another moment. She couldn't remember the last time the air here had sizzled with so much energy. Letting out a long breath, she bent to pick up her gardening tools, while Quigley wound himself around her legs.

She certainly couldn't remember the last time her palms had gone damp just because a man had looked at her.

Then again, she couldn't recall ever being looked at in quite that way before. Looked at, looked into, looked through, all at once. A very neat trick, she mused as she carried the tools into her greenhouse.

An intriguing pair, father and daughter. Gazing through the sparkling glass wall of the greenhouse, she studied the house centered in the next yard. As their closest neighbor, she thought, it was only natural that she should wonder about them. Ana was also wise enough—and had learned through painful experience—to be careful not to let her wondering lead to any involvement beyond a natural friendliness.

There were precious few who could accept what was not of the common world. The price of her gift was a vulnerable heart that had already suffered miserably at the cold hand of rejection.

But she didn't dwell on that. In fact, as she thought of the man, and of the child, she smiled. What would he have done, she wondered with a little laugh, if she had told him that, while she wasn't an ogre—no, indeed—she was most definitely a witch.

In the sunny and painfully disorganized kitchen, Boone Sawyer dug through a packing box until he unearthed a skillet. He knew the move to California had been a good one—he'd convinced himself of that—but he'd certainly underestimated the time, the trouble and the general inconvenience of packing up a home and plopping it down somewhere else.

What to take, what to leave behind. Hiring movers, having his car shipped, transporting the puppy that Jessie had fallen in love with. Justifying his decision to her worried grandparents, school registration—school shopping. Lord, was he going to have to repeat that nightmare every fall for the next eleven years?

At least the worst was behind him. He hoped. All he had to do now was unpack, find a place for everything and make a home out of a strange house.

Jessie was happy. That was, and always had been, the most important thing. Then again, he mused as he browned some beef for chili, Jessie was happy anywhere. Her sunny disposition and her remarkable capacity to make friends were both a blessing and a bafflement. It was astonishing to Boone that a child who had lost her mother at the tender age of two could be unaffected, so resilient, so completely normal.

And he knew that if not for Jessie he would surely have gone quietly mad after Alice's death.

He didn't often think of Alice now, and that fact sometimes brought him a rush of guilt. He had loved her—God, he had loved her—and the child they'd made together was a living, breathing testament to that love. But he'd been without her now longer than he'd been with her. Though he had tried to hang on to the grief, as a kind of proof of that love, it had faded under the demands and pressures of day-to-day living.

Alice was gone, Jessie was not. It was because of both of them that he'd made the difficult decision to move to Monterey. In Indiana, in the home he and Alice had bought while she was carrying Jessie, there had been too many ties to the past. Both his parents and Alice's had been a ten-minute drive away. As the only grandchild on both sides, Jessie had been the center of attention, and the object of subtle competition.

For himself, Boone had wearied of the constant advice, the gentle—and not so gentle—criticism of his parenting. And, of course, the matchmaking. The child needs a mother. A man needs a wife. His mother had decided to make it her life's work to find the perfect woman to fit both bills.

Because that had begun to infuriate him, and because he'd realized how easy it would be to stay in the house and wallow in the memories it held, he'd chosen to move.

He could work anywhere. Monterey had been the final choice because of the climate, the life-style, the schools. And, he could admit privately, because some internal voice had told him this was the place. For both of them.

He liked being able to look out of the window and see the water, or those fascinatingly sculptured cypress trees. He certainly liked the fact that he wasn't crowded in by neighbors. It was Alice who had enjoyed being surrounded by people. He also appreciated the fact that the distance from the road was enough to muffle the sound of traffic.

It just felt right. Jessie was already making her mark. True, it had given him a moment of gut-clutching fear when he'd looked outside and hadn't seen her anywhere. But he should have known she would find someone to talk to, someone to charm.

And the woman.

Frowning, Boone settled the top on the skillet to let the chili simmer. That had been odd, he thought as he poured a cup of coffee to take out on the deck. He'd looked down at her and known instantly that Jessie was safe. There had been nothing but kindness in those smoky eyes. It was his reaction, his very personal, very basic reaction, that had tightened his muscles and roughened his voice.

Desire. Very swift, very painful, and totally inappropriate. He hadn't felt that kind of response to a woman since... He grinned to himself. Since never. With Alice it had been a quiet kind of rightness, a sweet and inevitable coming together that he would always treasure.

This had been like being dragged by an undertow when you were fighting to get to shore.

Well, it had been a long time, he reminded himself as he watched a gull glide toward the water. A healthy reaction to a beautiful woman was easily justified and explained. And beautiful she'd been, in a calm, classic manner that was the direct opposite of his violent response to her. He couldn't help but resent it. He didn't have the time or inclination for any kind of reaction to any kind of woman.

There was Jessie to think of.

Reaching in his pocket, he took out a cigarette, lit it, hardly aware he was staring across the lawn at the hedge of delicate roses.

Anastasia, he thought. The name certainly suited her. It was old-fashioned, elegant, unusual.

"Daddy!"

Boone jolted, as guilty as a teenager caught smoking in the boys' room by the high school principal. He cleared his throat and gave his pouting daughter a sheepish grin.

"Give your old man a break, Jess. I'm down to half a pack a day."

She folded her arms. "They're bad for you. They make your lungs dirty."

"I know." He tamped the cigarette out, unable to take even a last drag when those wise little eyes were judging him. "I'm giving them up. Really."

She smiled—it was a disconcertingly adult sure-you-are smile—and he jammed his hands in his pockets. "Give me a break, Warden," he said in a passable James Cagney imitation. "You ain't putting me in solitary for snitching one drag."

Giggling, already forgiving him for the lapse, she came over to hug him. "You're silly."

"Yeah." He cupped his hands under her elbows and lifted her up for a hearty kiss. "And you're short."

"One day I'm going to be big as you." She wrapped her legs around his waist and leaned back until she was upside down. It was one of her favorite pastimes.

"Fat chance." He held her steady as her hair brushed the deck. "I'm always going to be bigger." He pulled her up again, lifting her high and making her squeal with laughter. "And smarter, and stronger." He rubbed the stubble of his beard against her while she wriggled and shrieked. "And better-looking."

"And ticklish!" she shouted in triumph, digging her fingers into his ribs.

She had him there. He collapsed on the bench with her. "Okay, okay! Uncle!" He caught his breath, and caught her close. "You'll always be trickier."

Pink-cheeked, bright-eyed, she bounced on his lap. "I like our new house."

"Yeah?" He smoothed her hair, as always enjoying the texture of it under his palm. "Me too."

"After dinner, can we go down to the beach and look for seals?"

"Sure."

"Daisy, too?"

"Daisy, too." Already experienced with puddles on the rug and chewed-up socks, he glanced around. "Where is she?"

"She's taking a nap." Jessie rested her head against her father's chest. "She was very tired."

"I bet. It's been a big day." Smiling, he kissed the top of Jessie's head, felt her yawn and settle.

"My favorite day. I got to meet Ana." Because her eyes were heavy, she closed them, lulled by the beating of her father's heart. "She's nice. She's going to show me how to plant flowers."

"Hmm."

"She knows all their names." Jessie yawned again, and when she spoke again her voice was thick with sleep. "Daisy licked her face and she didn't even mind. She just laughed. It sounded pretty when she did. Like a fairy," Jessie murmured as she drifted off.

Boone smiled again. His daughter's imagination. His gift to her, he liked to think. He held her gently while she slept.

Restless, Ana thought as she strolled along the rocky beach at twilight. She simply wasn't able to stay inside, working with her plants and herbs, when she was dogged by this feeling of restlessness.

The breeze would blow it out of her, she decided, lifting her face to the moist wind. A nice long walk and she'd find that contentment again, that peace that was as much a part of her as breathing.

Under different circumstances she would have called one of her cousins and suggested a night out. But she imagined Morgana was cozily settled in with Nash for the evening. And at this stage of her pregnancy, she needed rest. Sebastian wasn't back from his honeymoon yet.

Still, it had never bothered her to be alone. She enjoyed the solitude of the long, curved beach, the sound of water against rock, the laughing of the gulls.

Just as she had enjoyed the sound of the child's laughter, and the man's, drifting to her that afternoon. It had been a good sound, one she didn't have to be a part of to appreciate.

Now, as the sun melted, spilling color over the western sky, she felt the restlessness fading. How could she be anything but content to be here, alone, watching the magic of a day at rest?

She climbed up to stand on a driftwood log, close enough to the water that the spray cooled her face and dampened her shirt. Absently she took a stone out of her pocket, rubbing it between her fingers as she watched the sun drop into the flaming sea.

The stone warmed in her hand. Ana looked down at the small, waterlike gem, its pearly sheen glinting dully in the lowering light. Moonstone, she thought, amused at herself. Moon magic. A protection for the night traveler, an aid to self-analysis. And, of course, a talisman, often used to promote love.

Which was she looking for tonight?

Even as she laughed at herself and slipped the stone back into her pocket, she heard her name called.

There was Jessie, racing down the beach with the fat puppy nipping at her heels. And her father, walking several yards behind, as if reluctant to close the distance. Ana took a moment to wonder if the child's natural exuberance made the man appear all the more aloof.

She stepped down from the log and, because it was natural, even automatic, caught Jessie up in a swing and a hug. "Hello again, sunshine. Are you and Daisy out hunting for faerie shells?"

Jessie's eyes widened. "Faerie shells? What do they look like?"

"Just as you'd suppose. Sunset or sunrise—that's the only time to find them."

"My daddy says faeries live in the forest, and usually hide because people don't always know how to treat them."

"Quite right." She laughed and set the girl on her feet. "But they like the water, too, and the hills."

"I'd like to meet one, but Daddy says they hardly ever talk to people like they used to 'cause nobody really believes in them but kids."

"That's because children are very close to magic." She looked up as she spoke. Boone had reached them, and the sun setting at his back cast shadows over his face that were both dangerous and appealing. "We were discussing faeries," she told him.

"I heard." He laid a hand on Jessie's shoulder. Though the gesture was subtle, the meaning was crystal-clear. *Mine.*

"Ana says there are faerie shells on the beach, and you can only find them at sunrise or sunset. Can you write a story about them?"

"Who knows?" His smile was soft and loving for his daughter. When his gaze snapped back to hers, Ana felt a shudder down her spine. "We've interrupted your walk."

"No." Exasperated, Ana shrugged. She understood that he meant she had interrupted theirs. "I was just taking a moment to watch the water before I went in. It's getting chilly.''

"We had chili for dinner," Jessie said, grinning at her own joke. "And it was *hot!* Will you help me look for faerie shells?"

"Sometime, maybe." When her father wasn't around to stare holes through her. "But it's getting too dark now, and I have to go in." She flicked a finger down Jessie's nose. "Good night." She gave a cool nod to her father.

Boone watched Ana walk away. She might not have gotten chilled so quickly, he thought, if she'd worn something to cover her legs. Her smooth, shapely legs. He let out a long, impatient breath.

"Come on, Jess. Race you back."

Chapter Two

"I'd like to meet him."

Ana glanced up from the dried petals she was arranging for potpourri and frowned at Morgana. "Who?"

"The father of this little girl you're so enchanted with." More fatigued than she cared to admit, Morgana stroked her hand in a circular motion over her very round belly. "You're just chock-full of information on the girl, and very suspiciously lacking when it comes to Papa."

"Because he doesn't interest me as much," Ana said lightly. To a bowl filled with fragrant leaves and petals she added lemon for zest and balsam for health. She knew very well how weary Morgana was. "He's every bit as standoffish as Jessie is friendly. If it wasn't obvious that he's devoted to her, I'd probably dislike him instead of being merely ambivalent."

"Is he attractive?"

Ana lifted a brow. "As compared to?"

"A toad." Morgana laughed and leaned forward. "Come on, Ana. Give."

"Well, he isn't ugly." Setting the bowl aside, she began to look through the cupboard for the right oil to mix through the potpourri. "I guess you'd say he has that hollow-cheeked, dangerous look. Athletic build. Not like a weight lifter." She frowned, trying to decide between two oils. "More like a . . . a long-distance runner, I suppose. Rangy, and intimidatingly fit."

Grinning, Morgana cupped her chin in her hands. "More."

"This from a married woman about to give birth to twins?"

"You bet."

Ana laughed, chose an oil of rose to add elegance. "Well, if I have to say something nice, he does have wonderful eyes. Very clear, very blue. When they look at Jessie, they're gorgeous. When they look at me, suspicious."

"What in the world for?"

"I haven't a clue."

Morgana shook her head and rolled her eyes. "Anastasia, surely you've wondered enough to find out. All you'd have to do is peek."

With a deft and expert hand, Ana added drops of fragrant oil to the mixture in the bowl. "You know I don't like to intrude."

"Oh, really."

"And if I was curious," she added, fighting a smile at Morgana's frustration, "I don't believe I'd care to see what was rolling around inside Mr. Sawyer's heart.

I have a feeling it would be very uncomfortable to be linked with him, even for a few minutes."

"You're the empath," Morgana said with a shrug. "If Sebastian was back, he'd find out what's in this guy's mind anyway." She sipped more of the soothing elixir Ana had mixed for her. "I could do it for you if you like. I haven't had cause to use the scrying mirror or crystal for weeks. I may be getting stale."

"No." Ana leaned forward and kissed her cousin's cheek. "Thank you. Now, I want you to keep a bag of this with you," she said as she spooned the potpourri into a net bag. "And put the rest in bowls around the house and the shop. You're only working two days a week now, right?"

"Two or three." She smiled at Ana's concern, even as she waved it off. "I'm not overdoing, darling, I promise. Nash won't let me."

With an absent nod, Ana tied the bag securely. "Are you drinking the tea I made up for you?"

"Every day. And, yes, I'm using the oils religiously. I'm carrying rhyolite to alleviate emotional stress, topaz against external stresses, zircon for a positive attitude and amber to lift my spirits." She gave Ana's hand a quick squeeze. "I've got all the bases covered."

"I'm entitled to fuss." She set the bag of potpourri down by Morgana's purse, then changed her mind and opened the purse herself to slip it inside. "It's our first baby."

"Babies," Morgana corrected.

"All the more reason to fuss. Twins come early."

Indulging in a single sigh, Morgana closed her eyes. "I certainly hope these do. It's getting to the point where I can hardly get up and down without a crane."

"More rest," Ana prescribed, "and very gentle exercise. Which does not include hauling around shipping boxes or being on your feet all day waiting on customers."

"Yes, ma'am."

"Now let's have a look." Gently she laid her hands on her cousin's belly, spreading 'her fingers slowly, opening herself to the miracle of what lay within.

Instantly Morgana felt her fatigue drain away and a physical and emotional well-being take its place. Through her half-closed eyes she saw Ana's darken to the color of pewter and fix on a vision only Ana could see.

As she moved her hands over her cousin's heavy belly and linked with her, Ana felt the weight within her and, for one incredibly vivid moment, the lives that pulsed inside the womb. The draining fatigue, yes, and the nagging discomfort, but she also felt the quiet satisfaction, the burgeoning excitement, and the simple wonder of carrying those lives. Her body ached, her heart swelled. Her lips curved.

Then she *was* those lives—first one, then the other. Swimming dreamlessly in that warm, dark womb, nourished by the mother, held safe and fast until the moment when the outside would be faced. Two healthy hearts beating steady and close, beneath a mother's heart. Tiny fingers flexing, a lazy kick. The rippling of life.

Ana came back to herself, came back alone. "You're well. All of you."

"I know." Morgana twined her fingers with Ana's. "But I feel better when you tell me. Just as I feel safe knowing you'll be there when it's time."

"You know I wouldn't be anywhere else." She brought their joined hands to her cheek. "But is Nash content with me as midwife?"

"He trusts you—as much as I do."

Ana's gaze softened. "You're lucky, Morgana, to have found a man who accepts, understands, even appreciates, what you are."

"I know. To have found love was precious enough. But to have found love with him." Then her smile faded. "Ana, darling, Robert was a long time ago."

"I don't think of him. At least not really of him, but of a wrong turn on a particularly slippery road."

Indignation sharpened Morgana's eyes. "He was a fool, and not in the least worthy of you."

Rather than sadness Ana felt a chuckle bubble out of her. "You never liked him. Not from the first."

"No, I didn't." Frowning, Morgana gestured with her glass. "And neither did Sebastian, if you recall."

"I do. As I recall Sebastian was quite suspicious of Nash, too."

"That was entirely different. It *was,*" she insisted as Ana grinned. "With Nash, he was just being protective of me. As for Robert, Sebastian tolerated him with the most insulting sort of politeness."

"I remember." Ana shrugged. "Which, of course, put my back up. Well, I was young," she said with a careless gesture. "And naive enough to believe that if I was in love I must be loved back equally. Foolish enough to be honest. And foolish enough to be devastated when that honesty was rewarded with disbelief, then outright rejection."

"I know you were hurt, but there's little doubt you could do better."

"None at all," Ana agreed, for she wasn't without pride. "But there are some of us that aren't meant to mix with outsiders."

Now there was frustration, as well as indignation. "There have been plenty of men, with elfin blood and without, who've been interested in you, cousin."

"A pity I haven't been interested in them." Ana laughed. "I'm miserably choosy, Morgana. And I like my life just as it is."

"If I didn't know that to be true, I'd be tempted to work up a nice little love spell. Nothing binding, mind," she said with a glint in her eye. "Just something to give you some entertainment."

"I can find my own entertainment, thanks."

"I know that, too. Just as I know you'd be furious if I dared to interfere." She pushed away from the table and rose, regretting for a moment her loss of grace. "Let's take a walk outside before I head home."

"If you promise to put your feet up for an hour when you get there."

"Done."

The sun was warm, the breeze balmy. Both of which, Ana thought, would do her cousin as much good as the long nap she imagined Nash would insist his wife take when she returned home.

They admired the late-blooming larkspur, the starry asters and the big, bold zinnias. Both had a deep love of nature that had come through the blood and through upbringing.

"Do you have any plans for All Hallows' Eve?" Morgana asked.

"Nothing specific."

"We were hoping you'd come by, at least for part of the evening. Nash is going all out for the trick-or-treaters."

With an appreciative laugh, Ana clipped some mums to take inside. "When a man writes horror films for a living, he's duty bound to pull out the stops for Halloween. I wouldn't miss it."

"Good. Perhaps Sebastian will join you and me for a quiet celebration afterward." Morgana was bending awkwardly over the thyme and verbena when she spotted the child and dog skipping through the hedge of roses.

She straightened. "We have company."

"Jessie." Pleased but wary, Ana glanced over to the house beyond. "Does your father know where you are?"

"He said I could come over if I saw you outside and you weren't busy. You aren't busy, are you?"

"No." Unable to resist, Ana bent down to kiss Jessie's cheek. "This is my cousin, Morgana. I've told her you're my brand-new neighbor."

"You have a dog and a cat. Ana told me." Jessie's interest was immediately piqued. Then her gaze focused, fascinated, on the bulge of Morgana's belly. "Do you have a baby in there?"

"I certainly do. In fact, I have two babies in there."

"Two?" Jessie's eyes popped wide. "How do you know?"

"Because Ana told me." With a laugh, she laid a hand on her heavy stomach. "And because they kick and squirm too much to be only one."

"My friend Missy's mommy, Mrs. Lopez, had one baby in her tummy, and she got so fat she could hardly walk." Out of brilliant blue eyes, Jessie shot Morgana a hopeful glance. "She let me feel it kick."

Charmed, Morgana took Jessie's hand and brought it to her while Ana discouraged Daisy from digging in the impatiens. "Feel that?"

Giggling at the movement beneath her hand, Jessie nodded. "Uh-huh! It went pow! Does it hurt?"

"No."

"Do you think they'll come out soon?"

"I'm hoping."

"Daddy says babies know when to come out because an angel whispers in their ear."

Sawyer might be aloof, Morgana thought, but he was also very clever, and very sweet. "That sounds exactly right to me."

"And that's their special angel, forever and ever," she went on, pressing her cheek to Morgana's belly in the hope that she could hear something from inside. "If you turn around really quick, you maybe could get just a tiny glimpse of your angel. I try sometimes, but I'm not fast enough." She peered up at Morgana. "Angels are shy, you know."

"So I've heard."

"I'm not." She pressed a kiss to Morgana's belly before she danced away. "There's not a shy bone in my body. That's what Grandma Sawyer always says."

"An observant woman, Grandma Sawyer," Ana commented while wrestling Daisy into her arms to prevent her from disturbing Quigley's afternoon nap.

Both women enjoyed the energetic company as they walked among the flowers—or rather as they walked and Jessie skipped, hopped, ran and tumbled.

Jessie reached for Ana's hand as they started toward the front of the house and Morgana's car. "I don't have any cousins. Is it nice?"

"Yes, it's very nice. Morgana and Sebastian and I practically grew up together, kind of like brothers and sisters do."

"I know how to get brothers and sisters, 'cause my daddy told me. How do you get cousins?"

"Well, if your mother or father have brothers or sisters, and they have children, those children are your cousins."

Jessie digested this information with a frown of concentration. "Which are you?"

"It's complicated," Morgana said with a laugh, opting to rest against her car for a moment before getting in. "Ana's and Sebastian's and my father are all brothers. And our mothers are sisters. So we're kind of double cousins."

"That's neat. If I can't have cousins, maybe I can have a brother or sister. But my daddy says I'm a handful all by myself."

"I'm sure he's right," Morgana agreed as Ana chuckled. Brushing her hair back, Morgana glanced up. There, framed in one of the wide windows on the second floor of the house next door, was a man. Undoubtedly Jessie's father.

Ana had described him well enough, Morgana mused. Though he was more attractive, and certainly sexier, than her cousin had let on. That very simple omission made her smile. Morgana lifted a hand in a friendly wave. After a moment's hesitation, Boone returned the salute.

"That's my daddy." Jessie pinwheeled her arms in greeting. "He works up there, but we haven't unpacked all the boxes yet."

"What does he do?" Morgana asked, since it was clear Ana wasn't going to.

"Oh, he tells stories. Really good stories, about witches and fairy princesses and dragons and magic fountains. I get to help sometimes. I have to go because tomorrow's my first day of school and he said I wasn't supposed to stay too long. Did I?"

"No." Ana bent down to kiss her cheek. "You can come back anytime."

"Bye!" And she was off, gamboling across the lawn, with the dog racing behind her.

"I've never been more charmed, or more worn out," Morgana said as she climbed into her car. "The girl's a delightful whirlwind." Smiling out at Ana, she jiggled her keys. "And the father is certainly no slouch."

"I imagine it's difficult, a man raising a little girl alone."

"From the one glimpse I had, he looked up to it." She gunned the engine. "Interesting that he writes stories. About witches and dragons and such. Sawyer, you said?"

"Yes." Ana blew tousled hair out of her eyes. "I guess he must be Boone Sawyer."

"It might intrigue him to know you're Bryna Donovan's niece—seeing as they're in the same line of work. That is, if you wanted to intrigue him."

"I don't," Ana said firmly.

"Ah, well, perhaps you already have." Morgana put the car in reverse. "Blessed be, cousin."

Ana struggled with a frown as Morgana backed out of the drive.

After driving to Sebastian's to give his horses their morning feeding and grooming, Ana spent most of the next morning delivering her potpourris, her scented oils, her medicinal herbs and potions. Others were boxed and packaged for shipping. Though she had several local customers for her wares, including Morgana's shop, Wicca, a great portion of her clientele was outside the area.

Anastasia's was successful enough to suit her. The business she'd started six years before satisfied her needs and ambitions and allowed her the luxury of working at home. It wasn't for money. The Donovan fortune, and the Donovan legacy, kept both her and her family comfortably off. But, like Morgana with her shop and Sebastian with his many businesses, Ana needed to be productive.

She was a healer. But it was impossible to heal everyone. Long ago she had learned it was destructive to attempt to take on the ills and pains of the world. Part of the price of her power was knowing there was pain she could not alleviate. She did not reject her gift. She used it as she thought best.

Herbalism had always fascinated her, and she accepted the fact that she had the touch. Centuries before, she might have been the village wise woman—and that never failed to amuse her. In today's world, she was a businesswoman who could mix a bath oil or an elixir with equal skill.

If she added a touch of magic, it was hers to add.

And she was happy, happy with the destiny that had been thrust on her and with the life she had made from it.

Even if she'd been miserable, she thought, this day would have lifted her spirits. The beckoning sun, the caressing breeze, the faintest taste of rain in the air, rain that would not fall for hours—and then would fall gently.

Wanting to take advantage of the day, she decided to work outside, starting some herbs from seed.

He was watching her again. Bad habit, Boone thought with a grimace as he glanced down at the cigarette between his fingers. He wasn't having much luck with breaking bad habits. Nor was he getting a hell of a lot of work done since he'd looked out of the window and had seen her outside.

She always looked so…elegant, he decided. A kind of inner elegance that wasn't the least diminished by the grass-stained cutoffs and short-sleeved T-shirt she wore.

It was in the way she moved, as if the air were wine that she drank lightly from as she passed through it.

Getting lyrical, he mused, and reminded himself to save it for his books.

Maybe it was because she was the fairy-princess type he so often wrote about. There was that ethereal, otherworldly air about her. And the quiet strength in her eyes. Boone had never believed that fairy princesses were pushovers.

But there was still this delicacy about her body—a body he sincerely wished he hadn't begun to dwell upon. Not a frailty, but a serene kind of femininity that he imagined would baffle and allure any male who was still breathing.

Boone Sawyer was definitely breathing.

Now what was she doing? he wondered, crushing out his cigarette impatiently and moving closer to the window. She'd gone into the garden shed and had come out again with her arms piled high with pots.

Wasn't it just like a woman to try to carry more than she should?

Even as he was thinking it, and indulging in a spot of male superiority, he saw Daisy streak across her lawn, chasing the sleek gray cat.

He had a hand on the window, prepared to shoot it up and call off the dog. Before he could make the move, he saw it was already too late.

In slow motion, it might have been an interesting and well-choreographed dance. The cat streaked like gray smoke between Ana's legs. She swayed. The clay pots in her arms teetered. Boone swore, then let out a sigh of relief when she righted them, and herself, again. Before the breath was out, Daisy plowed through, destroying the temporary balance. This time Ana's feet were knocked completely out from under her. She went down, and the pots went up.

Though he was already swearing, Boone heard the crash as he leapt through the terrace doors and down the steps to the lower deck.

She was muttering what sounded to him like exotic curses when he reached her. And he could hardly blame her. Her cat was up a tree, spitting down on the yipping dog. The pots she'd been carrying were little more than shards scattered over the grass and the edge of the patio where the impact had taken place.

Boone winced, cleared his throat. "Ah, are you all right?"

She was on her hands and knees, and her hair was over her eyes. But she tossed it back and shot him a long look through the blond wisps. "Dandy."

"I was at the window." This certainly wasn't the time to admit he'd been watching her. "Passing by the window," he corrected. "I saw the chase and collision." Crouching down, he began to help her pick up the pieces. "I'm really sorry about Daisy. We've only had her a few days, and we haven't had any luck with training."

"She's a baby yet. No point in blaming a dog for doing what comes naturally."

"I'll replace the pots," he said, feeling miserably awkward.

"I have more." Because the barking and spitting were getting desperate, Ana sat back on her heels. "Daisy!" The command was quiet but firm, and it was answered instantly. Tail wagging furiously, the pup scrambled over to lick at her face and arms. Refusing to be charmed, Ana cupped the dog's face in her hands. "Sit," she ordered, and the puppy plopped her rump down obligingly. "Now behave yourself." With a little whine of repentance, Daisy settled down with her head on her paws.

Almost as impressed as he was baffled, Boone shook his head. "How'd you do that?"

"Magic," she said shortly, then relented with a faint smile. "You could say I've always had a way with animals. She's just happy and excited and roaring to play. You have to make her understand that some activities are inappropriate." Ana patted Daisy's head and earned an adoring canine glance.

"I've been trying bribery."

"That's good, too." She stretched out under a trellis of scarlet clematis, looking for more broken crockery. It was then that Boone noticed the long scratch on her arm.

"You're bleeding."

She glanced down. There were nicks on her thighs, too. "Hard to avoid, with pots raining down on me."

He was on his feet in a blink and hauling Ana to hers. "Damn it, I asked you if you were all right."

"Well, really, I—"

"We'll have to clean it up." He saw there was more blood trickling down her legs, and he reacted exactly as he would if it were Jessie. He panicked. "Oh, Lord." He scooped an amazed Ana into his arms and hurried toward the closest door.

"Honestly, there's absolutely no need—"

"It's going to be fine, baby. We'll take care of it."

Half amused, half annoyed, Ana huffed out a breath as he pushed his way into the kitchen. "In that case, I'll cancel the ambulance. If you'd just put me—" He dropped her into one of the padded ice-cream chairs at her kitchen table. "Down."

Nerves jittering, Boone raced to the sink for a cloth. Efficiency, speed and cheer were the watchwords in such cases, he knew. As he dampened the cloth and squirted it with soap, he took several long breaths to calm himself.

"It won't look so bad when we get it cleaned up. You'll see." After pasting a smile on his face, he walked back to kneel in front of her. "I'm not going to hurt you." Gently he began to dab at the thin line of blood that had dripped down her calf. "We're going to fix it right up. Just close your eyes and relax."

He took another long breath. "I knew this man once," he began, improvising a story as he always did for his daughter. "He lived in a place called Briarwood, where there was an enchanted castle behind a high stone wall."

Ana, who had been on the point of firmly telling him she could tend to herself, stopped and did indeed relax.

"Growing over the wall were thick vines with big, razor-sharp thorns. No one had been to the castle in more than a hundred years, because no one was brave enough to climb that wall and risk being scraped and pricked. But the man, who was very poor and lived alone, was curious, and day after day he would walk from his house to the wall and stand on the tips of his toes to see the sun gleam on the topmost towers and turrets of the castle."

Boone turned the cloth over and dabbed at the cuts. "He couldn't explain to anyone what he felt inside his heart whenever he stood there. He wanted desperately to climb over. Sometimes at night in his bed he would imagine it. Fear of those thick, sharp thorns stopped him, until one day in high summer, when the scent of flowers was so strong you couldn't take a breath without drinking it in, that glimpse of the topmost towers wasn't enough. Something in his heart told him that what he wanted most in the world lay just beyond that thorn-covered wall. So he began to climb it. Again and again he fell to the ground, with his hands and arms pricked and bleeding. And again and again he pushed himself up."

His voice was soothing, and his touch—his touch was anything but. As gentle as he was with the cool cloth, an ache began to spread, slow and warm, from the center of her body outward. He was stroking her thighs now, where the sharp edge of a shard had nicked the flesh. Ana closed her hand into a fist, the twin of which clenched in her stomach.

She needed him to stop. She wanted him to go on. And on.

"It took all of that day," Boone continued in that rich, mesmerizing storyteller's voice. "And the heat mixed sweat with the blood, but he didn't give up. Couldn't give up, because he knew, as he'd never known anything before, that his heart's desire, his future and his destiny, lay on the other side. So, with his hands raw and bleeding, he used those thorny vines and dragged himself to the top. Exhausted, filled with pain, he stumbled and fell down and down, to the thick, soft grass that flowed from the wall to the enchanted castle.

"The moon was up when he awoke, dazed and disoriented. With the last of his strength, he limped across the lawn, over the drawbridge and into the great hall of the castle that had haunted his dreams since childhood. When he crossed the threshold, the lights of a thousand torches flared. In that same instant, all his cuts and scrapes and bruises vanished. In that circle of flame that cast shadow and light up the white marble walls stood the most beautiful woman he had ever seen. Her hair was like sunlight, and her eyes like smoke. Even before she spoke, even before her lovely mouth curved in a welcoming smile, he knew that it was she he had risked his life to find. She stepped forward, offered her hand to him, and said only, 'I have been waiting for you.'"

As he spoke the last words, Boone lifted his gaze to Ana's. He was as dazed and disoriented as the man in the story he had conjured up. When had his heart begun to pound like this? he wondered. How could he think when the blood was swimming in his head and throbbing in his loins? While he struggled for balance, he stared at her.

Hair like sunlight. Eyes like smoke.

And he realized he was kneeling between her legs, one hand resting intimately high on her thigh, and the other on the verge of reaching out to touch that sunlight hair.

Boone rose so quickly that he nearly overbalanced the table. "I beg your pardon," he said, for lack of anything better. When she only continued to stare at him, the pulse in her throat beating visibly, he tried again. "I got carried away when I saw you were bleeding. I've never been able to take Jessie's cuts and scrapes in stride." Struggling not to babble, he thrust the cloth at her. "I imagine you'd rather handle it yourself."

She accepted the cloth. She needed a moment before she dared speak. How was it possible that a man could stir her so desperately with doctoring and a fairy tale, then leave her fighting to find a slippery hold on her composure when he apologized?

Her own fault, Ana thought as she scrubbed—with more force than was really necessary—at the scrape on her arm. It was her gift and her curse that she would feel too much.

"You look like you should be the one sitting down," she told him briskly, then rose to go to the cupboard for one of her own medications. "Would you like something cold to drink?"

"No... Yes, actually." Though he doubted that a gallon of ice water would dampen the fire in his gut. "Blood always makes me panic."

"Panicked or not, you were certainly efficient." She poured him a glass of lemonade from the fat pitcher she fetched from the refrigerator. "And it was a very nice story." She was smiling now, more at ease.

"A story usually serves to calm both Jessie and me during a session with iodine and bandages."

"Iodine stings." She expertly dabbed a tobacco-brown liquid from a small apothecary jar onto her cleaned cuts. "I can give you something that won't, if you like. For your next emergency."

"What is it?" Suspicious, he sniffed at the jar. "Smells like flowers." And so did she.

"For the most part it is. Herbs, flowers, a dash of this and that." She set the bottle aside, capped it. "It's what you might call a natural antiseptic. I'm an herbalist."

"Oh."

She laughed at the skeptical look on his face. "That's all right. The majority of people only trust healing aids they can buy at the drugstore. They forget that people healed themselves quite well through nature for hundreds of years."

"They also died of lockjaw from a nick from a rusty nail."

"True enough," she agreed. "If they didn't have access to a reputable healer." Since she had no intention of trying to convert him, Ana changed the subject. "Did Jessie get off for her first day of school?"

"Yeah, she was raring to go. I was the one with the nervous stomach." His smile came and went. "I want to thank you for being so tolerant of her. I know she has a tendency to latch on to people. It doesn't cross her mind that they might not want to entertain her.''

"Oh, but she entertains me." In an automatic gesture of courtesy, she took out a plate and lined it with cookies. "She's very welcome here. She's very sweet, unaffected and bright, and she doesn't forget her manners. You're doing a marvelous job raising her."

He accepted a cookie, watching her warily. "Jessie makes it easy."

"As delightful as she is, it can't be easy raising a child on your own. I doubt it's a snap even with two parents when the child is as energetic as Jessie. And as bright." Ana selected a cookie for herself and missed the narrowing of his eyes. "She must get her imagination from you. It must be delightful for her to have a father who writes such lovely stories."

His eyes sharpened. "How do you know what I do?"

The suspicion surprised her, but she smiled again. "I'm a fan—actually, an avid fan—of Boone Sawyer's."

"I don't recall telling you my first name."

"No, I don't believe you did," Ana said agreeably. "Are you always so suspicious of a compliment, Mr. Sawyer?"

"I had my reasons for settling quietly here." He set the half-empty glass down on the counter with a little clink. "I don't care for the idea of my neighbor interrogating my daughter, or digging into my business."

"Interrogating?" She nearly choked on the word. "Interrogating Jessie? Why would I?"

"To get to know a little more about the rich widower in the next house."

For one throbbing moment, she could only gape. "How unbelievably arrogant! Believe me, I enjoy Jessie's company, and I don't find it necessary to bring you into the conversation."

What he considered her painfully transparent astonishment made him sneer. He'd handled her type before, but it was a disappointment, a damned disappointment, for Jessie. "Then it's odd that you'd know my name, that I'm a single parent, and my line of work, isn't it?"

She wasn't often angry. It simply wasn't her nature. But now she fought a short, vicious war with temper. "You know, I doubt very much you're worth an explanation, but I'm going to give you one, just to see how difficult it is for you to talk when you have to shove your other foot in your mouth." She turned. "Come with me."

"I don't want—"

"I said come with me." She strode out of the kitchen, fully certain he would follow.

Though annoyed and reluctant, he did. They moved through an archway and into a sun-drenched great room dotted with the charm of white wicker furniture and chintz. There were clusters of glinting crystals, charming statues of elves and sorcerers and faeries. Through another archway and into a cozy library with a small Adam fireplace and more mystical statuary.

There was a deep cushioned sofa in raspberry that would welcome an afternoon napper, daintily feminine lace curtains dancing in the breeze that teased through an arching window, and the good smell of books mixed with the airy fragrance of flowers.

Ana walked directly to a shelf, rising automatically to her toes to reach the desired volumes. *"The Milk-*

maid's Wish,'' she recited as she pulled out one book after another. *"The Frog, the Owl and the Fox. A Third Wish for Miranda.''* She tossed a look over her shoulder, though tossing one of the books would have been more satisfactory. "It's a shame I have to tell you how much I enjoy your work."

Uncomfortable, he tucked his hands in his pockets. He was already certain he'd taken a wrong turn, and he was wondering if he could find a suitable way to backtrack. "It isn't often grown women read fairy tales for pleasure."

"What a pity. Though you hardly deserve the praise, I'll tell you that your work is lyrical and valuable, on both a child's and an adult's level." Far from mollified, she shoved two of the books back into place. "Then again, perhaps such things are in my blood. I was very often lulled to sleep by one of my aunt's stories. Bryna Donovan," she said, and had the pleasure of seeing his eyes widen. "I imagine you've heard of her."

Thoroughly chastised, Boone let out a long breath. "Your aunt." He flicked his gaze over the shelf and saw several of Bryna's stories of magic and enchanted lands alongside his. "We've actually corresponded a few times. I've admired her work for years."

"So have I. And when Jessie mentioned that her father wrote stories about fairy princesses and dragons, I concluded the Sawyer next door was Boone Sawyer. Grilling a six-year-old wasn't necessary."

"I'm sorry." No, actually, he was much more embarrassed than sorry, but that would have to do. "I had an... uncomfortable experience not long before we moved, and it's made me overly sensitive." He picked up a small, fluidly sculpted statue of an enchantress, turning it in his fingers as he spoke. "Jessie's kindergarten teacher...she pumped all sorts of information out of the kid. Which isn't too hard, really, since Jessie's pump's always primed."

He set the statue down again, all the more embarrassed that he felt this obligation to explain. "But she manipulated Jessie's feelings, her natural need for a mother figure, gave her all sorts of extra attention, requested several conferences to discuss Jessie's unusual potential, even going so far as to arrange a one-on-one with me over dinner where she... Suffice it to say she was more interested in an unattached male with a nice portfolio than she was in Jessie's feelings or her welfare. Jessie was very hurt by it."

Ana tapped a finger on the edge of one of his books before replacing it. "I imagine it was a difficult experience for both of you. But let me assure you, I'm not in the market for a husband. And, if I were, I wouldn't resort to manipulations and maneuvers. I'm afraid happy-ever-after has been too well indoctrinated in me for that."

"I'm sorry. After I get those feet out of my mouth, I'll try to come up with a better apology."

The way she lifted her brow told him he wasn't out of the woods yet. "I think the fact that we understand each other will do. Now I'm sure you want to get back to work, and so do I." She walked past him into a tiled foyer and opened the front door. "Tell Jessie to be sure to drop by and let me know how she likes school."

Here's your hat, what's your hurry, Boone thought as he stepped out. "I will. Take care of those scratches," he added, but she was already closing the door in his face.

Chapter Three

Good going, Sawyer. Shaking his head, Boone sat down in front of his word processor. First his dog knocks her down in her own yard, then our blundering hero barges into her house uninvited to play with her legs. To cap it, he insults her integrity and insinuates that she's using his daughter to try to trap him.

All in one fun-filled afternoon, he thought in disgust. It was a wonder she hadn't pitched him bodily out of her house rather than simply slamming the door in his face.

And why had he acted so stupidly? Past experience, true. But that wasn't the root of it, and he knew it.

Hormones, he decided with a half laugh. The kind of raging hormones better suited to a teenager than a grown man.

He'd looked up at her face in that sun-washed kitchen, feeling her skin warm under his hand, smelling that serenely seductive scent she exuded, and he'd wanted. He'd craved. For one blinding moment, he'd imagined with perfect clarity what it would be like to drag her off that curvy little chair, to feel that quick jerk-shudder of reaction as he devoured that incredibly soft-looking mouth.

That instant edge of desire had been so sharp, he'd needed to believe there was some outside force, some ploy or plot or plan to jumble his system so thoroughly.

Safest course, he realized with a sigh. Blame her.

Of course, he might have been able to dismiss the whole thing if it hadn't been for the fact that at that moment he'd looked up into her eyes and seen the same dreamy hunger he was feeling. And he'd felt the power, the mystery, the titanic sexuality, of a woman on the point of yielding.

His imagination had a great deal of punch, he knew. But what he'd seen, what he'd felt, had been utterly real.

For a moment, for just a moment, the tensions and needs had had that room humming like a harp string. Then he'd pulled back—as he should. A man had no business seducing his neighbor in her kitchen.

Now he'd very likely destroyed any chance of getting to know her better—just when he'd realized he very much wanted to get to know Miss Anastasia Donovan.

Pulling out a cigarette, Boone ran his fingers over it while he thought through various methods of redemption. When the light dawned, it was so simple he laughed out loud. If he'd been looking for a way into the fair maiden's heart—which he wasn't, exactly—it couldn't have been more perfect.

Pleased with himself, he settled down to work until it was time to pick up Jessie at school.

Conceited jerk. Ana worked off her temper with mortar and pestle. It was very satisfying to grind something—even if it was only some innocent herbs—into a powder. Imagine. *Imagine* him having the idea that she was...on the make, she decided, sneering. As if she'd found him irresistible. As if she'd been pining away behind some glass wall waiting for her prince to come. So that she could snare him.

The gall of the man.

At least she'd had the satisfaction of thumbing her nose at him. And if closing a door in anyone's face was out of character for her, well, it had felt wonderful at the time.

So wonderful, in fact, that she wouldn't mind doing it again.

It was a damn shame he was so talented. And it couldn't be denied that he was a wonderful father. They were traits she couldn't help but admire. There was no denying he was attractive, magnetically sexual, with just a dash of shyness tossed in for sweetness, along with the wild tang of untamed male.

And those eyes, those incredible eyes that just about stopped your breath when they focused on you.

Ana scowled and tightened her grip on the pestle. Not that she was interested in any of that.

There might have been a moment in the kitchen, when he was stroking her flesh so gently and his voice blocked out all other sound, that she found herself drawn to him.

All right, aroused by him, she admitted. It wasn't a crime.

But he'd certainly shut that switch off quickly enough, and that was fine by her.

Beginning this instant, and from now on, she would think of him only as Jessica's father. She would be aloof if it killed her, friendly only to the point where it eased her relationship with the child.

She enjoyed having Jessie in her life, and she wasn't about to sacrifice that pleasure because of a basic and very well justified dislike of Jessie's father.

"Hi!"

There was that pixie face peeping through Ana's screen door. Even the dregs of temper were difficult to hold on to when she was faced with those big smiling eyes.

Ana set the mortar and pestle aside and smiled back. She supposed she had to be grateful that Boone hadn't let the altercation that afternoon influence him to keep Jessie away.

"Well, it looks like you survived your first day of school. Did school survive you?"

"Uh-huh. My teacher's name is Mrs. Farrell. She has gray hair and big feet, but she's nice, too. And I met Marcie and Tod and Lydia and Frankie, and lots of others. In the morning we—"

"Whoa." With a laugh, Ana held up both hands. "Maybe you should come in and sit down before you give me the day's events."

"I can't open the door, 'cause my hands are full."

"Oh." Ana obligingly pushed open the screen. "What have you got there?"

"Presents." On a huff of breath, Jessie dropped a package on the table. Then she held up a large crayon drawing. "We got to draw pictures today, and I made two. One for Daddy and one for you."

"For me?" Touched, Ana accepted the colorful drawing on the thick beige paper that brought back some of her own school memories. "It's beautiful, sunshine."

"See, this is you." Jessie pointed out a figure with yellow hair. "And Quigley." Here a childish, but undeniably clever, depiction of a cat. "And all the flowers. The roses and the daisies and the lark things."

"Larkspur," Ana murmured, misty-eyed.

"Uh-huh. And all the others," Jessie continued. "I couldn't remember all the names. But you said you'd teach me."

"Yes, I will. It's just lovely, Jessie."

"I drew Daddy one of our new house with him standing out on the deck, because he likes to stand there best. He put it on the refrigerator."

"An excellent idea." Ana walked over to center the picture on the refrigerator door, anchoring it with magnets.

"I like to draw. My daddy draws real good, and he said my mommy drew even better. So I come by it naturally." Jessie slipped her hand into Ana's. "Are you mad at me?"

"No, sweetheart. Why would I be?"

"Daddy said Daisy knocked you down and broke your pots, and you got hurt." She studied the scratch on Ana's arm, then kissed it solemnly. "I'm sorry."

"It's all right. Daisy didn't mean it."

"She didn't mean to chew up Daddy's shoes, either, and make him say swear words."

Ana bit her lip. "I'm sure she didn't."

"Daddy yelled, and Daisy got so nervous she peed right on the rug. Then he chased her around and around the house, and it looked so funny that I couldn't stop laughing. And Daddy laughed, too. He said he was going to build a doghouse outside and put Daisy and me in it."

Ana lost any hope of taking it all seriously, and she laughed as she scooped Jessie up. "I think you and Daisy would have a great time in the doghouse. But if you'd like to save your father's shoes, why don't you let me help you work with her?"

"Do you know how? Can you teach her tricks and everything?"

"Oh, I imagine. Watch." She shifted Jessie to her hip and called Quigley out from his nap beneath the kitchen table. The cat rose reluctantly, stretched his front legs, then his back, then padded out. "Okay, sit." Heaving a feline sigh, he did. "Up." Resigned, Quigley rose on his haunches and pawed the air like a circus tiger. "Now, if you do your flip, I might just open a can of tuna fish later, for your dinner."

The cat seemed to be debating with himself. Then— perhaps because the trick was small potatoes compared to tuna—he leapt up, arching his back and flipping over to land lightly on his feet. While Jessie crowed with laughter and applauded, Quigley modestly cleaned his paws.

"I didn't know cats could do tricks."

"Quigley's a very special cat." Ana set Jessie down to give Quigley a stroking. He purred like a freight train, nuzzling his face against her knee. "His family's in Ireland, like most of mine."

"Does he get lonely?"

Smiling, Ana scratched under Quigley's jaw. "We have each other. Now, would you like a snack while you tell me about the rest of your day?"

Jessie hesitated, tempted. "I don't think I can, 'cause it's close to dinner, and Daddy— Oh, I almost forgot." She rushed back to the table to pick up a package wrapped in candy-striped paper. "This is for you, from Daddy."

"From..." Unconsciously Ana linked her hands behind her back. "What is it?"

"I know." Jessie grinned, her eyes snapping with excitement. "But I can't tell. Telling spoils the surprise. You have to open it." Jessie picked it up and thrust it at Ana. "Don't you like presents?" Jessie asked when Ana kept her hands clasped tight behind her back. "I like them best of anything, and Daddy always gives really good ones."

"I'm sure he does, but I—"

"Don't you like Daddy?" Jessie's lower lip poked out. "Are you mad at him because Daisy broke your pots?"

"No, no, I'm not mad at him." Not for the broken pots, anyway. "It wasn't his fault. And, yes, of course I like him— That is, I don't know him very well, and I..." Caught, Ana decided, and she worked up a smile. "I'm just surprised to get a present when it's not my birthday." To please the child, Ana took the gift and shook it. "Doesn't rattle," she said, and Jessie clapped and giggled.

"Guess! Guess what it is!"

"Ah... a trombone?"

"No, no, trombones are too big." Excitement had her bouncing. "Open it. Open it and see."

It was the child's reaction that had her own heart beating a shade too fast, Ana assured herself. To please Jessie, she ripped the paper with a flourish. "Oh."

It was a book, a child's oversize book with a snowy white cover. On the front was a beautiful illustration of a golden-haired woman wearing a sparkling crown and flowing blue robes.

"The Faerie Queen," Ana read. "By Boone Sawyer."

"It's brand-new," Jessie told her. "You can't even buy it yet, but Daddy gets his copies early." She ran a hand gently over the picture. "I told him she looks like you."

"It's a lovely gift," Ana said with a sigh. And a sneaky one. How was she supposed to stay irritated with him now?

"He wrote something inside for you." Too impatient to wait, Jessie opened the cover herself. "See, right there."

To Anastasia, with hopes that a magic tale works as well as a white flag. Boone.

Her lips curved. It was impossible to prevent it. How could anyone refuse a truce so charmingly requested?

Which was, of course, what Boone was counting on. As he shoved a packing box out of his way with his foot, he glanced through the window toward the house next door. Not a peep.

He imagined it might take a few days for Ana to calm down, but he thought he'd made a giant stride in the right direction. After all, he didn't want any antagonism between himself and Jessie's new friend.

Turning back to the stove, he lowered the heat on the boneless chicken breasts he had simmering, then deftly began to mash potatoes.

Jessie's number one favorite he thought, as he sent the beaters whirling. They could have mashed potatoes every night for a year and the kid wouldn't complain. Of course, it was up to him to vary the menu, to make sure she got a healthy meal every night.

Boone poured in more milk and grimaced. He had to admit, if there was one part of parenting he would cheerfully give up, it was the pressure of deciding what they were to eat night after night.

He didn't mind cooking it so much, it was that daily decision between pot roast, baked chicken, pork chops and all the others. Plus what to serve with it. Out of desperation, he'd begun to clip recipes—secretly—in hopes of adding some variety.

At one time he'd seriously considered hiring a housekeeper. Both his mother and his mother-in-law had urged him to, and then they'd gone into one of their competitive huddles on how to choose the proper woman to fit the bill. But the idea of having someone in the house, someone who might gradually take over the rearing of his daughter, had deterred him.

Jessie was his. One hundred percent his. Despite dinner decisions and grocery shopping, that was the way he liked it.

As he added a generous slice of butter to the creamy potatoes, he heard her footsteps racing across the deck.

"Good timing, frog face. I was just about to give you a whistle." He turned, licking potatoes from his finger and saw Ana standing in the doorway, one hand on Jessie's shoulder. The muscles in his stomach tightened so quickly that he nearly winced. "Well, hello."

"I didn't mean to interrupt your cooking," Ana began. "I just wanted to thank you for the book. It was very nice of you to send it over."

"I'm glad you like it." He realized he had a dishcloth tucked in his jeans and hastily tugged it out. "It was the best peace offering I could think of."

"It worked." She smiled, charmed by the sight of him hovering busily over a hot stove. "Thanks for thinking of me. Now, I'd better get out of your way so you can finish cooking your dinner."

"She can come in, can't she?" Jessie was already tugging on Ana's hand. "Can't she, Daddy?"

"Sure. Please." He shoved a box out of her way. "We haven't finished unpacking yet. It's taking longer than I thought it would."

Out of politeness, and curiosity, Ana stepped inside. There were no curtains on the window as yet, and a few packing boxes littered the stone colored floor tiles. But ranged along the royal blue countertop there was a glossy ceramic cookie jar in the shape of Alice's white rabbit, a teapot of the mad hatter, and a dormouse sugar bowl. Potholders, obviously hooked by a child's hand, hung on little brass hooks. The refrigerator's art gallery was crowded with Jessie's drawings, and the puppy was snoozing in the corner.

Unpacked and tidy, no, she thought. But this was already a home.

"It's a great house," she commented. "I wasn't surprised when it sold quickly."

"You want to see my room?" Jessie tugged on Ana's hand again. "I have a bed with a roof on it, and lots of stuffed animals."

"You can take Ana up later," Boone put in. "Now you should go wash your hands."

"Okay." She looked imploringly at Ana. "Don't go."

"How about a glass of wine?" Boone offered when his daughter raced off. "A good way to seal a truce."

"All right." Drawings rustled as he opened the fridge. "Jessie's quite an artist. It was awfully sweet of her to draw a picture for me."

"Careful, or you'll have to start papering the walls with them." He hesitated, the bottle in his hand, wondering where he'd put the wineglasses, or if he'd unpacked them at all. A quick search through cupboards made it clear that he hadn't. "Can you handle chardonnay in a Bugs Bunny glass?"

She laughed. "Absolutely." She waited for him to pour hers, and his—Elmer Fudd. "Welcome to Monterey," she said, raising Bugs in a toast.

"Thanks." When she lifted the glass to her lips and smiled at him over the rim, he lost his train of thought. "I . . . Have you lived here long?"

"All my life, on and off." The scent of simmering chicken and the cheerful disarray of the kitchen were so homey that she relaxed. "My parents had a home here, and one in Ireland. They're based in Ireland for the most part now, but my cousins and I settled here. Morgana was born in the house she lives in, on Seventeen Mile Drive. Sebastian and I were born in Ireland, in Castle Donovan."

"Castle Donovan."

She laughed a little. "It sounds pretentious. But it actually is a castle, quite old, quite lovely, and quite remote. It's been in the Donovan family for centuries."

"Born in an Irish castle," he mused. "Maybe that explains why the first time I saw you I thought, well, there's the faerie queen, right next door in the rose-bushes." His smiled faded, and he spoke without thinking. "You took my breath away."

The glass stopped halfway to her lips. Those lips parted in surprised confusion. "I ..." She drank to give herself a moment to think. "I suppose part of your gift would be imagining faeries under bushes, elves in the garden, wizards in the treetops."

"I suppose." She smelled as lovely as the breeze that brought traces of her garden and hints of the sea through his windows. He stepped closer, surprised and not entirely displeased to see the alarm in her eyes. "How's that scratch? Neighbor." Gently he cupped his hand around her arm, skimmed his thumb up until he felt the pulse inside her elbow skitter. Whatever was affecting him was damn well doing the same to her. His lips curved. "Hurt?"

"No." Her voice thickened, baffling her, arousing him. "No, of course it doesn't."

"You still smell of flowers."

"The salve—"

"No." The knuckles of his free hand skimmed just under her chin. "You always smell of flowers. Wild-flowers and sea foam."

How had she come to be backed against the counter, his body brushing hers, his mouth so close, so tempt-ingly close, that she could all but taste it?

And she wanted that taste, wanted it with a sudden staggering force that wiped every other thought out of her head. Slowly, her eyes on his, she brought her hand to his chest, spread it over his heart where the beat was strong. Strong and wild.

And so would the kiss be, she thought. Strong and wild, from the first instant.

As if to assure her of that, he grabbed a fistful of her hair, tangling his fingers in it. It was warm, as he'd known it would be, warm as the sunlight it took its shade from. For a moment, his entire being was focused on the kiss to come, the reckless pleasure of it. His mouth was a breath from hers, and her sigh was already filling him, when he heard his daughter's feet clattering on the stairs.

Boone jolted back as if she'd burned him. Speechless, they stared at each other, both of them stunned by what had nearly happened and by the force behind it.

What was he doing? Boone asked himself. Grabbing a woman in his kitchen when there was chicken on the stove, potatoes going cold on the counter and his little girl about to skip into the room?

"I should go." Ana set down her glass before it could slip out of her trembling hand. "I really only meant to stay a minute."

"Ana." He shifted, blocking the way in case she sprinted for the door. "I have a feeling what just happened here was out of character for both of us. That's interesting, don't you think?"

She lifted those solemn gray eyes to his. "I don't know your character."

"Well, I don't make a habit of seducing women in the kitchen when my daughter's upstairs. And I certainly don't make a habit out of wanting the hell out of a woman the minute I lay eyes on her."

She wished she hadn't set the wine down. Her throat was bone dry. "I suppose you want me to say I'll take your word for it. But I won't."

Both anger and challenge sparkled in his eyes. "Then I'll have to prove it to you, won't I?"

"No, you—"

"My hands are clean, clean, clean." Blissfully unaware of the tension shimmering in the air, Jessie danced into the kitchen, palms held out for inspection. "How come they have to be clean when I don't eat with my fingers anyway?"

Effortfully, he pulled himself back and tweaked his daughter's nose. "Because germs like to sneak off little girls' hands and into their mashed potatoes."

"Yuck." She made a face, then grinned. "Daddy makes the best mashed potatoes in the whole wide world. Don't you want some? She can stay for dinner, can't she, Daddy?"

"Really, I—"

"Of course she can." Mirroring his daughter's grin—but with something a great deal more dangerous in his eyes—Boone studied Ana. "We'd love to have you. We have plenty. And I think it would be a good idea for us to get to know each other. Before."

She didn't have to ask before what. That was crystal-clear. But, no matter how she tried, she couldn't make her temper overtake the quick panicked excitement. "It's very nice of you to ask," she said with admirable calm. "I wish I could, but—" She smiled down at Jessie's sound of disappointment. "I have to drive out to my cousin's and take care of his horses."

"Will you take me with you sometime, so I can see them?"

"If your father says it's all right." She bent down and kissed Jessie's sulky lips. "Thank you for my picture, sunshine. It's beautiful." Taking a cautious step away, she looked at Boone. "And the book. I know I'll enjoy it. Good night."

Ana didn't run out of the house, though she freely admitted she wasn't leaving so much as escaping. Back home, she went through the motions, giving Quigley his promised tuna, then changing into jeans and a denim shirt for the drive to Sebastian's house.

She was going to have to do some thinking, she decided as she pulled on her boots. Some serious thinking. Weigh the pros and cons, consider the consequences. She had to laugh, thinking how Morgana would roll her eyes and accuse her of being impossibly Libran.

Perhaps her birth sign was partially responsible for the fact that Ana could always see and sympathize with both sides of an argument. It complicated matters as often as it solved them. But in this case she was quite certain that a clear head and calm deliberation was the order of the day.

Maybe she was unusually attracted to Boone. And the physical aspect of it was completely unprecedented. Certainly she'd felt desire for a man before, but never this quick, sharp edge of it. And a sharp edge usually meant a deep wound to follow.

That was certainly something to consider. Frowning, she grabbed a jean jacket and started downstairs.

Of course, she was an adult, unattached, unencumbered, and perfectly free to entertain the thought of a relationship with an equally free adult man.

Then again, she knew just how devastating relationships could be when people were unable to accept others for what they were.

Still debating, she swung out of the house. She certainly didn't owe Boone any explanations. She was under no obligation to try to make him understand her heritage, as she had tried to do years before with Robert. Even if they became involved, she wouldn't have to tell him.

Ana got into her car and backed out of the drive, her thoughts shifting back and forth.

It wasn't deception to hold part of yourself back. It was self-preservation—as she'd learned through hard experience. And it was foolish even to be considering that angle when she hadn't decided if she wanted to be involved.

No, that wasn't quite true. She wanted. It was more a matter of deciding if she could afford to become involved.

He was, after all, her neighbor. A relationship gone sour would make it very uncomfortable when they lived in such close proximity.

And there was Jessie to consider. She was half in love with the girl already. She wouldn't want to risk that friendship and affection by indulging her own needs. Purely physical needs, Ana told herself as she followed the winding road along the coast.

True, Boone would be able to offer her some physical pleasure. She didn't doubt that for a moment. But the emotional cost would just be too steep for everyone involved.

It would be better, much better, for everyone involved if she remained Jessie's friend while maintaining a wise distance from Jessie's father.

Dinner was over, and the dishes were done. There had been a not-too-successful session with Daisy—though she would sit down if you pushed on her rump. Afterward, there'd been a lot of splashing in the tub, then some horseplay to indulge in with his freshly scrubbed daughter. There was a story to be told, that last glass of water to be fetched.

Once Jessie was asleep and the house was quiet, Boone indulged himself with a brandy out on the deck. There were piles of forms on his desk—a parent's homework—that had to be filled out for Jessie's school files.

He'd do them before he turned in, he decided. But this hour, this dark, quiet hour when the nearly full moon was rising, was his.

He could enjoy the clouds that were drifting overhead, promising rain, the hypnotic sound of the water lapping against rock, the chatter of insects in the grass that he would have to mow very soon, and the scent of night-blooming flowers.

No wonder he had snapped this house up at the very first glimpse. No place he'd ever been had relaxed him more, or given him more of a sense of rightness and peace. And it appealed to his imagination. The mystically shaped cypress, the magical ice plants that covered the banks, those empty and often eerie stretches of night beach.

The ethereally beautiful woman next door.

He smiled to himself. For someone who hadn't felt much more than an occasional twinge for a woman in too long to remember, he was certainly feeling a barrage of them now.

It had taken him a long time to get over Alice. Though he still didn't consider himself part of the dating pool, he hadn't been a monk over the past couple of years. His life wasn't empty, and he'd been able, after a great deal of pain, to accept the fact that he had to live it.

He was sipping his brandy, enjoying it and the simple pleasure of the night, when he heard Ana's car. Not that he'd been waiting for it, Boone assured himself even as he checked his watch. He couldn't quite smother the satisfaction at her being home early, too early to have gone out on a date.

Not that her social life was any of his business.

He couldn't see her driveway, but because the night was calm he heard her shut her car door. Then, a few moments later, he heard her open and close the door to her house.

Propping his bare feet on the rail of the deck, he tried to imagine her progress through the house. Into the kitchen. Yes, the light snapped on, and he could see her move past the window. Brewing tea, perhaps, or pouring herself a glass of wine.

Shortly, the light switched off again, and he let his mind follow her through the house. Up the stairs. More lights, but it looked to Boone like the glow of a candle against the dark glass, rather than a lamp. Moments later, he heard the faint drift of music. Harp strings. Haunting, romantic, and somehow sad.

Briefly, very briefly, she was silhouetted against a window. He could see quite clearly that slim feminine shadow as she stripped out of her shirt.

Hastily he swallowed brandy and looked away. However tempting it might be, he wouldn't lower himself to the level of a Peeping Tom. He did, however, find himself craving a cigarette, and with apologies to his disapproving daughter he pulled one out of his pocket.

Smoke stung the air, soothed his nerves. Boone contented himself with the sound of harpsong.

It was a very long time before he went back into the house and slept, with the sound of a gentle rain falling on the roof and the memory of harpsong drifting across the night breeze.

Chapter Four

Cannery Row was alive with sounds, the chattering of people as they strolled or rushed, the bright ringing of a bell from one of the tourist bikes, the ubiquitous calling of gulls searching for a handout. Ana enjoyed the crowds and the noise as much as she enjoyed the peace and solitude of her own backyard.

Patiently she chugged along with the stream of weekend traffic. On her first pass by Morgana's shop, Ana resigned herself to the fact that the perfect day had brought tourists and locals out in droves. Parking was going to be at a premium. Rather than frustrate herself searching for a spot on the street, she pulled into a lot three blocks from Wicca.

As she climbed out to open her trunk, she heard the whine of a cranky toddler and the frustrated muttering of weary parents.

''If you don't stop that right this minute, you won't get anything at all. I mean it, Timothy. We've had just about enough. Now get moving.''

The child's response to that command was to go limp, sliding in a boneless heap onto the parking lot as his mother tugged uselessly at his watery arms. Ana bit her lip as it curved, but it was obvious the young parents didn't see the humor of it. Their arms were full of packages, and their faces were thunderous.

Timothy, Ana thought, was about to get a tanning—though it was unlikely to make him more cooperative. Daddy shoved his bags at Mommy and, mouth grim, bent down.

It was a small thing, Ana thought. And they all looked so tired and unhappy. She made the link first with the father, felt the love, the anger, and the dark embarrassment. Then with the child—confusion, fatigue, and a deep unhappiness over a big stuffed elephant he'd seen in a shop window and been denied.

Ana closed her eyes. The father's hand swung back as he prepared to administer a sharp slap to the boy's diaper-padded rump. The boy sucked in his breath, ready to emit a piercing wail at the indignity of it.

Suddenly the father sighed, and his hand fell back to his side. Timothy peeked up, his face hot and pink and tear-streaked.

The father crouched down, holding out his arms. ''We're tired, aren't we?''

On a hiccuping sob, Timothy bundled into them and rested his heavy head on his daddy's shoulder. ''Thirsty.''

''Okay, champ.'' The father's hand went to the child's bottom, but with a soothing pat. He gave his teary-eyed wife an encouraging smile. "Why don't we go have a nice, cold drink? He just needs a n-a-p."

They moved off, tired but relieved.

Smiling to herself, Ana unlocked her trunk. Family vacations, she thought, weren't all fun and frolic. The next time they were ready to snarl at each other, she wouldn't be around to help. She imagined they'd muddle through without her.

After swinging her purse behind her back, she began to unload the boxes she was delivering to Morgana. There were a half dozen of them, filled with sacks of potpourri, bottles of oils and creams, beribboned sachets, satiny sleep pillows and a month's supply of special orders that ran from tonics to personalized perfumes.

Ana considered making two trips, gauged the distance and decided that if she balanced the load carefully she could make it in one.

She stacked, juggled and adjusted, then just managed to shut her trunk with an elbow. She made it across the parking lot and down half a block before she began berating herself.

Why did she always do this? she asked herself. Two comfortable trips were better than one difficult one. It wasn't that the boxes were so heavy—though they were. It was simply that they were awkward and the sidewalk was jammed. And her hair was blowing in her eyes. With a quick, agile dance, she managed, barely, to avoid a collision with a couple of teenage tourists in a surrey.

"Want some help?"

Annoyed with herself and irresponsible drivers, she turned around. There was Boone, looking particularly wonderful in baggy cotton slacks and shirt. Riding atop his shoulders, Jessie was laughing and clapping her hands.

"We had a ride on the carousel and had ice cream and we saw you."

"Looks like you're still overloading," Boone commented.

"They're not heavy."

He patted Jessie's leg and, following the signal, she began to slide down his back. "We'll give you a hand."

"That's all right." She knew it was foolish to reject help when she needed it, but she had managed quite successfully to avoid Boone for the better part of a week. And had managed—almost as successfully—to avoid thinking about him. Wondering about him. "I don't want to take you out of your way."

"We're not going any way in particular, are we, Jessie?"

"Uh-uh. We're just wandering today. It's our day off."

Ana couldn't prevent the smile, any more than she could prevent the wariness from creeping into her eyes when she looked back at Boone. He was certainly looking at her, she realized, in that disconcertingly thorough way of his. The smile creeping around his mouth had less to do with humor than it did with challenge.

"I don't have to go far," she began, grabbing at a package that was beginning to slide. "I can just—"

"Fine." Overriding her objections, Boone shifted boxes from her arms to his. His eyes stayed on hers. "What are neighbors for?"

"I can carry one." Eager to help, Jessie bounced in her sneakers. "I can."

"Thank you." Ana handed Jessie the lightest box. "I'm going a couple of blocks down to my cousin's shop."

"Has she had her babies?" Jessie asked as they started to walk.

"No, not yet."

"I asked Daddy how come she got to have two in there, and he said sometimes there's twice the love."

How could anyone possibly have a defense against a man like this? Ana wondered. Her eyes were warm when they met his. "Yes, sometimes there is. You always seem to have the right answer," she murmured to Boone.

"Not always." He wasn't certain if he was relieved or annoyed that his hands were full of boxes. If they'd been free, he would have been compelled to touch her. "You just try for the best one at the time. Where have you been hiding, Anastasia?"

"Hiding?" The warmth fled from her eyes.

"I haven't seen you out in your yard in days. You didn't strike me as the type to scare that easily."

Because Jessie was skipping just ahead of them, she bit off a more acid response. "I don't know what you mean. I had work. Quite a bit of it, as a matter of fact." She nodded toward the boxes. "You're carrying some of it now."

"Is that so? Then I'm glad I didn't resort to knocking on your door and pretending I needed to borrow a cup of sugar. I nearly did, but it seemed so obvious."

She slanted him a look. "I appreciate your restraint."

"And so you should."

She merely tossed her hair out of her eyes and called to Jessie. "We'll go down this way, so we can go in the back. Saturdays are usually busy," she explained to Boone. "I don't like going through the shop and distracting the customers."

"What does she sell, anyway?"

"Oh." Ana smiled again. "This and that. I think you'd find her wares particularly interesting. Here we go." She gestured to a little flagstone stoop flanked by pots of bloodred geraniums. "Can you get the door, Jessie?"

"Okay." Anxious as ever to see what was on the other side, Jessie shoved it open, then let out a squeal. "Oh, look. Daddy, look!" Jessie set her package aside on the first available space and made a dive for the big white cat grooming herself on the table.

"Jessica!" Boone's voice was short and firm, stopping his daughter in midstride. "What have I told you about going up to strange animals?"

"But, Daddy, he's so pretty."

"She," Ana corrected as she laid her boxes on the counter. "And your father's quite right. Not all animals like little girls."

Jessie's fingers itched to stroke the thick white fur. "Does she?"

"Sometimes Luna doesn't like anyone." With a laugh, Ana scratched the cat between the ears. "But if you're very polite, and pet her when she gives the royal consent, you'll get along well enough." Ana gave Boone a reassuring smile. "Luna won't scratch her. When she's had enough, she'll just stalk off."

But apparently Luna was in the mood for attention. Walking to the end of the table, she rubbed her head against the hand Jessie had held out. "She likes me!'' The smile nearly split her face in two. ''See, Daddy, she likes me.''

''Yes, I see.''

''Morgana usually keeps cold drinks back here.'' Ana opened the small refrigerator. ''Would you like something?''

''Sure.'' He really wasn't thirsty, but the offer made it easy to linger. He leaned back against the counter of the kitchenette while Ana got out glasses. ''The shop through there?''

When he gestured at a door, Ana nodded. ''Yes. And through there's the storeroom. A great deal of what Morgana sells is one-of-a-kind, so she doesn't keep a large supply of inventory.''

He reached over Ana's shoulder to finger the thin leaves of a rosemary plant on the windowsill. ''She into this kind of thing, too?''

Ana tried to ignore the fact that his body was brushing hers. She could smell the sea on him, and imagined he and Jessie had gone down to feed the gulls. ''What kind of thing?''

''Herbs and stuff.''

''In a manner of speaking.'' She turned, knowing she'd be entirely too close, and pushed the glass into his chest. ''Root beer.''

''Terrific.'' He knew it wasn't particularly fair—and it was probably unwise, as well—but he took the glass and stood precisely where he was. She had to tilt her head back to meet his eyes. ''It might be a good hobby for Jessie and me. Maybe you could show us how to grow some.''

''It's no different from growing any living thing.'' It took a great deal of effort to keep her voice even when breathing was so difficult. "Care and attention, and affection. You're very much in my way, Boone."

"I hope so." With his eyes very intense, very focused, he lifted a hand to her cheek. "Anastasia, I really think we need to—"

"A deal's a deal, babe." The smug voice carried through the door as it opened. "Fifteen minutes of sit-down time every two hours."

"You're being ridiculous. For heaven's sake, you act as though I'm the only pregnant woman in the world." Heaving a sigh, Morgana walked into the back room. Her brows lifted when she saw the trio—and particularly when she saw the way Boone Sawyer was caging her cousin at the rear counter.

"You're the only pregnant woman in my world." Nash stopped short. "Hey, Ana, you're just the woman I need to convince Morgana to take it easy. Now that you're here, I can…" He glanced once at the man beside her, then back again to focus. "Boone? Well, I'll be damned. Boone Sawyer, you son of a—" He caught himself, mostly because Morgana shot an elbow into his ribs. There was a little girl, all eyes, standing at the table. "Gun," he finished, and strode across the room to shake Boone's hand and slap his back in a typical male greeting. "What are you doing here?"

"Delivering stock, I think." He grinned, gripping Nash's hand hard in his. "How about you?"

"Trying to keep my wife in line. Lord, what's it been? Four years?"

"Just about."

Morgana folded her hands on her belly. "I take it you two know each other?"

"Sure we do. Boone and I met at a writers' conference. It has to be ten years ago, doesn't it? I haven't seen you since—" Since Alice's funeral, Nash remembered abruptly. And he remembered, too, the devastation, the despair and the disbelief in Boone's eyes as he'd stood beside his wife's grave. "How are you?"

"Okay." Understanding, Boone smiled. "We're okay."

"Good." Nash put a hand on Boone's shoulder and squeezed before he turned to Jessie. "And you're Jessica."

"Uh-huh." She beamed up at him, always interested in meeting someone new. "Who are you?"

"I'm Nash." He crossed to her, crouched down. Except for the eyes, eyes that were all Boone, she was the image of Alice. Bright, pretty, pixielike. He offered her a formal handshake. "It's nice to meet you."

She giggled and shook his hand. "Did you put the babies into Morgana?"

To his credit, he was speechless only for a moment. "Guilty." With a laugh, he picked her up. "But I'm leaving it up to Ana to get them out. So, what are the two of you doing in Monterey?"

"We live here now," Jessie told him. "Right next door to Ana's house."

"No kidding?" Nash grinned over at Boone. "When?"

"A little more than a week. I'd heard you'd moved here, and I figured I'd look you up once we got things together. I didn't realize you were married to my neighbor's cousin."

"A small and fascinating world, isn't it?" Morgana commented. She tilted her head at Ana, well aware that her cousin hadn't said a word since they'd come into the room. "Since no one's going to introduce me, I'm Morgana."

"Sorry," Nash said, jiggling Jessie on his hip. "Sit down."

"I'm perfectly—"

"Sit." This from Ana as she pulled out a chair.

"Outnumbered." Sighing, Morgana sat. "Are you enjoying Monterey?"

"Very much," Boone told her, and his gaze shifted to Ana. "More than I anticipated."

"I always enjoy having more than I anticipated." With a light laugh, she patted her belly. "We'll all have to get together very soon, so you can tell me things Nash doesn't want me to know."

"I'd be glad to."

"Babe, you know I'm an open book." He kissed the top of Morgana's head and winked at Ana. "That the stuff Morgana's been waiting for?"

"Yes, all of it." Anxious to keep her hands busy, Ana turned to the pile of boxes. "I'll unpack it for you. Morgana, I want you to try out this new violet body lotion before you put it out, and I brought extra of the soapwort shampoo."

"Good, I'm completely out." She took the bottle of lotion from Ana and unstopped the bottle. "Nice scent." She dabbed a bit on the back of her hand and rubbed it in. "Good texture."

"Sweet violets, and the Irish moss Da sent me." She glanced up from her unpacking. "Nash, why don't you show Jessie and Boone the shop?"

"Good idea. I think you're going to find a lot of this right up your alley," Nash told Boone as he led the way to the door.

Boone shot a look over his shoulder before he passed through. "Anastasia." He waited until she glanced up from the boxes. "Don't run away."

"My, my, my." Morgana settled back and smiled like a cat with a direct line to Bossy. "Want to fill me in?"

With a little more force than necessary, Ana ripped through packing tape. "On what?"

"On you and your gorgeous neighbor, of course."

"There's nothing to fill in."

"Darling, I know you. When I walked into this room, you were so wrapped up in him I could have called out a tornado and you wouldn't have blinked."

Ana busied herself unpacking bottles. "Don't be ridiculous. You haven't called out a tornado since the first time we saw *The Wizard of Oz.*"

"Ana." Morgana's voice was low and firm. "I love you."

"I know. I love you, too."

"You're never nervous. Perhaps that's why it's so fascinating—and concerning—to me that you're so nervous just now."

"I'm not." She rapped two bottles together and winced. "All right, all right, all right. I have to think about it." She whipped around. "He makes me nervous, and it would be ridiculous to deny it's the fact that I'm very attracted to him that's making me so nervous. I just have to think about it."

"Think about what?"

"How to handle it. Him, I mean. I have no intention of making another mistake, particularly since anything I do that involves Boone also involves Jessie."

"Oh, honey, are you falling in love with him?"

"That's absurd." Ana realized too late that the denial was too forceful to be taken at face value. "I'm just jumpy, that's all. I haven't had a man affect me like this, physically, in..." Ever. Never before, and, she was very much afraid, never again. "In a long time. I just need to think," she repeated.

"Ana." Morgana held out both hands. "Sebastian and Mel will be back in a couple of days from their honeymoon. Why don't you ask him to look? It would relieve your mind if you knew."

Resolute, Ana shook her head. "No...not that I haven't considered it. Whatever happens, however it happens, I want it to be on equal terms. Knowing would give me an unfair advantage over Boone. I have a feeling those equal terms would be important, to both of us."

"You know best. Let me tell you something, as a woman." Her lips curved. "As a witch. Knowing, not knowing, makes no difference with a man, once he touches your heart. No difference at all."

Ana nodded. "Then I'll have to make sure he doesn't touch mine until I'm ready."

"This is incredible," Boone was saying as he surveyed Wicca. "Just incredible."

"I thought so, too, the first time I walked in." Nash picked up a crystal wand tipped at the end with a spear of amethyst. "I guess people in our line of work are suckers for this stuff."

"Fairy tales," Boone agreed, accepting the wand before running a finger over a bronze cast of a snarling wolf. "Or the occult. A fine line between the two. Your last movie chilled my blood even when it made me laugh."

Nash grinned. "The humor in horror."

"Nobody does it better." He glanced over at his daughter. She was staring at a miniature silver castle surrounded by a moat of rainbow glass, her eyes huge, her hands behind her back. "I'll never get out of here empty-handed."

"She's beautiful," Nash said, wondering, as he often did, about the children that would be his before much longer.

"Looks like her mother." He saw the question and the concern in his friend's eyes. "Grief passes, Nash, whether you want it to or not. Alice was a wonderful part of my life, and she gave me the best thing in it. I'm grateful for every moment I had with her." He set the wand down. "Now I'd like to know how you—the world's most determined bachelor—came to be married and expecting twins."

"Research." Nash grinned and rocked back on his heels. "I wanted to get out of L.A., and keep within commuting distance. I'd only been here a short time when I needed to do some research on a script. I walked in here, and there she was."

There was more, of course. A great deal more. But it wasn't Nash's place to tell Boone about the Donovan legacy. Not even if Boone would have believed him.

"When you decide to take the plunge, you take it big."

"You, too. Indiana's a long way from here."

"I didn't want to be able to commute," Boone said with a grimace. "My parents, Alice's parents. Jessie and I were becoming their life's work. And I wanted a change, for both of us."

"Next door to Ana, huh?" Nash narrowed his eyes. "The redwood place, with all the glass and decks?"

"That's the one."

"Good choice." He glanced toward Jessie again. She'd wandered around the shop and had worked her way back to the little castle. She hadn't once asked for it, and that made the naked desire in her eyes all the more effective. "If you don't buy her that, I will."

When Ana came out to restock a few shelves for Morgana, she saw not only the silver castle being rung up on the counter, but the wand, a three-foot sculpture of a winged faerie she'd had her eye on herself, a crystal sun-catcher in the shape of a unicorn, a pewter wizard holding a many-faceted ball, and a baseball-sized geode.

"We're weak," Boone said with a quick, sheepish grin as Ana lifted a brow. "No willpower."

"But excellent taste." She ran a fingertip over the faerie wings. "Lovely, isn't she?"

"One of the best I've seen. I figured I'd put her in my office for inspiration."

"Good idea." She bent over a compartment containing tumbling stones. "Malachite, for clear thinking." Her fingers walked through the smooth stones, testing, rejecting, selecting. "Sodalite to relieve mental confusion, moonstone for sensitivity. Amethyst, of course, for intuition."

"Of course."

She ignored him. "A crystal for all-around good things." Tilting her head, she studied him. "Jessie says you're trying to quit smoking."

He shrugged. "I'm cutting down."

She handed him the crystal. "Keep it in your pocket. Tumbling stones are on the house." When she turned away with her colorful bottles, he picked up the crystal and rubbed it with his fingers.

It couldn't hurt.

He didn't believe in magic crystals or stone power— though he did think they had plot possibilities. Boone also had to admit they looked kind of nice in the little bowl on his desk. Atmosphere, he thought, like the geode he'd bought to use as a paperweight.

All in all, the afternoon had had several benefits. He and Jessie had enjoyed themselves thoroughly, riding the carousel at the Emporium, playing video games, just walking down Cannery Row and Fisherman's Wharf. Running into Anastasia had been a plus, he mused as he toyed with the creamy moonstone. And seeing Nash again, discovering that they lived in the same area, was gold.

He'd been missing male companionship. Funny, he hadn't realized it, as busy as his life had been over the past few months, with planning the move, executing the move, adjusting to the move. And Nash, though their friendship had primarily been through correspondence over the years, was exactly the kind of companion Boone preferred. Easygoing, loyal, imaginative.

It would be a kick to be able to pass on a few fatherly hints to Nash once his twins were born.

Oh, yeah, he reflected as he held up the moonstone, watching it gleam in the bright wash of moonlight through his office window, it certainly was a small and fascinating world.

One of his oldest friends, married to the cousin of the woman next door. It would certainly be hard for Anastasia to avoid him now.

And, no matter what she said, that was exactly what she'd been doing. He had a very strong feeling—and he couldn't help being a bit smug about it—that he was making the fair maiden nervous.

He'd nearly forgotten what it was like to approach a woman who reacted with faint blushes, confused eyes and rapid pulses. Most of the women he'd escorted over the past couple of years had been sleek and sophisticated—and safe, he added with a little shrug. He'd enjoyed their companionship, and he'd never lost his basic enjoyment of female company. But there'd been no tug, no mystery, no illusion.

He supposed he was still the kind of man attracted to the old-fashioned type. The roses-and-moonlight type, he thought with a half laugh. Then he saw her, and the laugh caught in his throat.

Down in her garden, walking, almost gliding through the silvery light, with the gray cat slipping in and out of the shadows. Her hair loose, sprinkling gold dust down her back and over the sheer shoulders of a pale blue robe. She carried a basket, and he thought he could hear her singing as she cut flowers and slipped them into it.

She was singing an old chant that had been passed down generation to generation. It was well past midnight, and Ana thought herself alone and unobserved. The first night of the full moon in autumn was the time to harvest, just as the first night of the full moon in spring was the time to sow. She had already cast the circle, purifying the area.

She laid the flowers and herbs in the basket as gently as children.

There was magic in her eyes. In her blood.

"Under the moon, through shadow and light, these blooms I chose by touch, by sight. Spells to weave to ease and free. As I will, so mote it be."

She plucked betony and heliotrope, dug mandrake root and selected tansy and balsam. Blood roses for strength, and sage for wisdom. The basket grew heavy and fragrant.

"Tonight to reap, tomorrow to sow. To take only that which I've caused to grow. Remembering always what is begun. To serve, to aid, an it harm none."

As the charm was cast, she lowered her face to the blooms, drawing in the ripe melody of the fragrance.

"I wondered if you were real."

Her head came up quickly, and she saw him, hardly more than a shadow by the hedge. Then he stepped through, into her garden, and became a man.

The heart that had leapt to her throat gradually settled again. "You startled me."

"I'm sorry." It must be the moonlight, he thought, that made her look so... enchanting. "I was working late, and I looked out and saw you. It seemed late to be picking flowers."

"There's a lot of moonlight." She smiled. He had seen nothing it wasn't safe for him to see. "I would think you'd know that anything picked under the full moon is charmed."

He returned the smile. "Got any rampion?"

The reference to Rapunzel made her laugh. "As a matter of fact, I do. No magic garden is complete without it. I'll pot some for you, if you like."

"I rarely say no to magic." The breeze fluttered her hair. Giving in to the moment, he reached out, took a handful. He watched the smile in her eyes fade. What replaced it had his blood singing.

"You should go in. Jessie's alone."

"She's asleep." He moved closer, as if the hair he'd twined around his finger were a rope and she were drawing him to her. He was within the circle now, within the magic she'd cast. "The windows are open, so I'd hear her if she called for me."

"It's late." Ana gripped the basket so tightly that the wicker dug into her skin. "I need to..."

Gently he took the basket and set it on the ground. "So do I." His other hand moved into her hair, combing it back from her face. "Very much."

As he lowered his mouth toward hers, she shivered and tried one last time to take control. "Boone, starting something like this could complicate things for all of us."

"Maybe I'm tired of things being simple." But he turned his head, just a fraction, so that his lips cruised up her cheek, over her temple. "I'm surprised you don't know that when a man finds a woman picking flowers in the moonlight he has no choice but to kiss her."

She felt her bones melting. Her body was pliant when she slipped into his arms. "And she has no choice but to want him to."

Her head fell back, and she offered. He thought he would take gently. The night seemed to call for it, with its perfumed breezes and the dreamy music of sea against rock. The woman in his arms was wand-slender, and the thin silk of her robe was cool over the warmth of satin skin.

But as he felt himself sink into that soft, lush mouth, as her fragrance whispered seductively around him, he dragged her hard against him and plundered.

Instantly desperate, instantly greedy. No rational thought could fight its way through the maze of sensations she brought to him. A sharp arrow of hunger pierced him, bringing on a groan that was only part pleasure.

Pain. He felt the aches of a thousand pricks of pain. Yet he couldn't pull himself away from her, couldn't stop his mouth from seeking more of hers. He was afraid, afraid that if he released her she would disappear like smoke—and he would never, never feel this way again.

She couldn't soothe him. Part of her wanted to stroke him and ease him and promise him that it would be all right, for both of them. But she couldn't. He devastated her. Whether it was her own grinding needs, the echo of his need seeping into her, or a mix of both, the result was a complete loss of will.

She had known, yes, she had known that this first meeting would be wild and strong. She'd craved it even as she'd feared it. Now she was beyond fear. Like him, she found the mixture of pain and pleasure irresistible.

Her trembling hands skimmed over his face, into his hair and locked there. Her body, shuddering from the onslaught, pressed urgently to his. When she murmured his name, she was breathless.

But he heard her, heard her through the blood pounding in his head, heard that soft, shaky sound. She was trembling—or he was. The uncertainty about who was more dazed had him slowly, carefully drawing away.

He held her still, his hands on her shoulders, his gaze on her face. In the moonlight, she could see herself there, trapped in that sea of blue. Trapped in him.

"Boone..."

"Not yet." He needed a moment to steady himself. By God, he'd nearly swallowed her whole. "Not just yet." Holding himself back, he touched his lips to hers, lightly, in a long, quiet kiss that wrecked whatever was left of her defenses. "I didn't mean to hurt you."

"You didn't." She pressed her lips together and tried to bring her voice over a whisper. "You didn't hurt me. You staggered me."

"I thought I was ready for this." He ran his hands down her arms before he released her. "I don't know if anyone could be." Because he wasn't sure what would happen if he touched her again, he slipped his hands into his pockets. "Maybe it's the moonlight, maybe it's just you. I have to be straight with you, Anastasia, I don't know quite how to handle this."

"Well." She wrapped her arms tight and cupped her elbows. "That makes two of us."

"If it wasn't for Jessie, you wouldn't go into that house alone tonight. And I don't take intimacy lightly."

Steadier now, she nodded. "If it wasn't for Jessie, I might ask you to stay with me tonight." She took a long breath. She knew it was important to be honest, at least in this. "You would be my first."

"Your—" His hands went limp. Now he felt both a lick of fear and an incredible excitement at the thought of her innocence. "Oh, God."

Her chin came up. "I'm not ashamed of it."

"No, I didn't mean..." Speechless, he dragged a hand through his hair. Innocent. A golden-haired virgin in a thin blue robe with flowers at her feet. And a man was supposed to resist, and walk away alone. "I don't suppose you have any idea what that does to a man."

"Not precisely, since I'm not a man." She bent down for her basket. "But I do know what realizing that you may soon be giving yourself for the first time does to a woman. So it seems to me we should both give this some clear thinking." She smiled, or tried to. "And it's very difficult to think clearly after midnight, when the moon's full and the flowers are ripe. I'll say good night, Boone."

"Ana." He touched her arm, but didn't hold on. "Nothing will happen until you're ready."

She shook her head. "Yes, it will. But nothing will happen unless it's meant."

With her robe billowing around her, she raced toward the house.

Chapter Five

Sleep had been a long time coming. Boone hadn't tossed and turned so much as lain, staring up at the ceiling. He'd watched the moonlight fade into that final deep darkness before dawn.

Now, with the sun streaming in bright ribbons over the bed, he was facedown, spread out, and fast asleep. In the dream floating through his brain, he scooped Ana into his arms and carried her up a long curved staircase of white marble. At the top, suspended above puffy, cotton clouds, was an enormous bed pooled in waterfalls of white satin. Hundreds of long, slender candles burned in a drifting light. He could smell them—the soft tang of vanilla, the mystique of jasmine. And her—that quietly sexy scent that went everywhere with her.

She smiled. Hair like sunlight. Eyes like smoke. When he laid her on the bed, they sank deep, as if into the clouds themselves. There was harpsong, romantic as tears, and a whisper that was nothing more than the clouds themselves breathing.

As her arms lifted, wound around him, they were floating, like ghosts in some fantasy, bound together by needs and knowledge and the unbearable sweetness of that first long, lingering kiss. Her mouth moved under his, yielding as she murmured . . .

"Daddy!"

Boone came awake with a crash as his daughter landed with a thump on his back. His unintelligible grunt had her giggling and scooting down to smack a kiss on his stubbled cheek.

"Daddy, wake up! I fixed you breakfast!"

"Breakfast." He grumbled into the pillow, struggling to clear the sleep from his throat and the dream from his system. "What time is it?"

"The little hand's on the ten, and the big hand's on the three. I made cinnamon toast and poured orange juice in the little glasses."

He grunted again, rolling over to peer through gritty eyes at Jessie. She looked bright as a sunbeam in her pink cotton blouse and shorts. She'd done the buttons up wrong, but she'd brushed the tangles from her hair. "How long have you been up?"

"Hours and hours and hours. I let Daisy outside and gave her breakfast. And I got dressed all by myself and brushed my teeth and watched cartoons. Then I got hungry, so I fixed breakfast."

"You've been busy."

"Uh-huh. And I was real quiet, too, so you didn't have to wake up early on your sleep-in day."

"You were real quiet," Boone agreed, and reached up to fix her buttons. "I guess you deserve a prize."

Her eyes lit. "What? What do I get?"

"How about a pink belly?" He rolled with her on the bed, wrestling while she squealed and wriggled. He let her win, pretending exhaustion and defeat when she bounced on his back. "Too tough for me."

"That's 'cause I eat my vegetables. You don't."

"I eat some."

"Uh-uh, hardly any."

"When you get to be thirty-three, you won't have to eat your brussels sprouts, either."

"But I like them."

He grinned into the pillow. "That's only because I'm such a good cook. My mother was lousy."

"She doesn't ever cook now." Jessie printed her name with a fingertip on her father's bare back. "Her and Grandpa Sawyer always go out to eat."

"That's because Grandpa Sawyer's no fool." She was having trouble with the letter *S*, Boone noted. They'd have to work on it.

"You said we could call Grandma and Grandpa Sawyer and Nana and Pop today. Can we?"

"Sure, in a couple of hours." He turned over again, studying her. "Do you miss them, baby?"

"Yeah." With her tongue between her teeth, she began to print *Sawyer* on his chest. "It seems funny that they're not here. Will they come to visit us?"

"Sure they will." The guilt that was part and parcel of parenthood worked at him. "Do you wish we'd stayed in Indiana?"

"No way!" Her eyes went huge. "We didn't have the beach there, and the seals and stuff, or the big carousel in town, or Ana living next door. This is the best place in the world."

"I like it here, too." He sat up and kissed her brow. "Now beat it, so I can get dressed."

"You'll come right downstairs for breakfast?" she asked as she slid from the bed.

"Absolutely. I'm so hungry I could eat a whole loaf of cinnamon toast."

Delighted, she rushed for the door. "I'm going to make more, right now."

Knowing she would take him at his word and go through an entire loaf of bread, Boone hurried through his shower, opted not to shave, and pulled on cutoffs and a T-shirt that would probably have done better in the rag pile.

He tried not to dwell on the dream. After all, it was simple enough to interpret. He wanted Ana—no big revelation there. And all that white—white on white— was obviously a symbol of her innocence.

It scared the hell out of him.

He found Jessie in the kitchen, busily slathering butter on another piece of toast. There was a plate heaped with them, more than a few of them burnt. The smell of cinnamon was everywhere.

Boone put on the coffee before he snagged a piece. It was cold, hard, and lumped with sugary cinnamon. Obviously, Jessie had inherited her grandmother's culinary talents.

"It's great," he told her, and swallowed gamely. "My favorite Sunday breakfast."

"Do you think Daisy can have some?"

Boone looked at the pile of toast again, glanced down at the pup, whose tongue was lolling out. With any luck he might be able to pawn off half his Sunday breakfast on the dog. "I think she could." Crouching, Boone held out a second piece of toast close enough for Daisy to sniff. "Sit," he ordered, in the firm, no-nonsense voice the training books had suggested.

Daisy continued to loll her tongue and wag her tail.

"Daisy, sit." He gave her rump a nudge. Daisy went down, then bounded back on all fours to jump at him. "Forget it." He held the toast out of reach and repeated the command. After five frustrating minutes—during which he tried not to remember how simple it had been for Ana—he managed to hold the dog's hindquarters down. Daisy gobbled up the bread, pleased with herself.

"She did it, Daddy."

"Sort of." He rose to pour himself some coffee. "We'll take her outside in a little while and have a real lesson."

"Okay." Jessie munched happily on her toast. "Maybe Ana's company will be gone, and she can help."

"Company?" Boone asked as he reached for a mug.

"I saw her outside with a man. She gave him a big hug and a kiss and everything."

"She—" The mug clattered onto the counter.

"Butterfingers," Jessie said, smiling.

"Yeah." Boone kept his back turned as he righted the mug and poured the coffee. "What, ah, sort of a man?" He thought his voice was casual enough—to fool a six-year-old, anyway.

"A really tall man with black hair. They were laughing and holding hands. Maybe it's her boyfriend."

"Boyfriend," Boone repeated between his teeth.

"What's the matter, Daddy?"

"Nothing. Coffee's hot." He sipped it black. Holding hands, he thought. Kissing. He'd get a look at this guy himself. "Why don't we go out on the deck, Jess? See if we can get Daisy to sit again."

"Okay." Singing the new song she'd learned in school, Jessie gathered up toast. "I like to eat outside. It's nice."

"Yeah, it's nice." Boone didn't sit when they were on the deck, but stood at the rail, the mug in his hand. He didn't see anyone in the next yard, and that was worse. Now he could imagine what Ana and her tall, dark-haired boyfriend might be doing inside.

Alone.

He ate three more pieces of toast, washing them down with black coffee while he fantasized about just what he'd say to Miss Anastasia Donovan the next time he saw her.

If she thought she could kiss him to the point of explosion one night, then dally with some strange guy the next morning, she was very much mistaken.

He'd straighten her out, all right. The minute he got ahold of her he'd—

His thoughts broke off when she came out the kitchen door, calling over her shoulder to someone.

"Ana!" Jessie leapt up on the bench, waving and shouting. "Ana, hi!"

While Boone watched through narrowed eyes, Ana looked in their direction. It seemed to him that her hand hesitated on its way up to return the wave, and her smile was strained.

Sure, he thought as he gulped down more coffee. I'd be nervous, too, if I had some strange man in the house.

"Can I go tell her what Daisy did? Can I, Daddy?"

"Yeah." His smile was grim as he set his empty mug on the rail. "Why don't you do that?"

Snatching up some more toast, she darted down the steps, calling for Daisy to follow and for Ana to wait.

Boone waited himself until he saw the man stroll outside to join Ana. He was tall, all right, Boone noted with some resentment. Several inches over six feet. He drew his own shoulders back. His hair was true black, and long enough to curl over his collar and blow—romantically, Boone imagined a woman would think—in the breeze.

He looked tanned, fit and elegant. And the breath hissed out between Boone's teeth when the stranger slipped an arm around Ana's shoulders as if it belonged there.

We'll see about this, Boone decided, and started down the deck stairs with his hands jammed in his pockets. We'll just see about this.

By the time he reached the hedge of roses, Jessie was already chattering a mile a minute about Daisy, and Ana was laughing, her arms tucked intimately around the stranger's waist.

"I'd sit, too, if someone was going to feed me cinnamon toast," the man said, and winked at Ana.

"You'd sit if anyone was going to feed you anything." Ana gave him a little squeeze before she noticed Boone at the hedge. "Oh." It was useless to curse the faint blush she felt heating her cheeks. "Good morning."

"How's it going?" Boone gave her a slow nod. Then his gaze moved suspiciously to the man beside her. "We didn't mean to interrupt while you have...company."

"No, that's all right, I—" She broke off, both confused and disconcerted by the tension humming in the air. "Sebastian, this is Jessie's father, Boone Sawyer. Boone, my cousin, Sebastian Donovan."

"Cousin?" Boone repeated, and Sebastian didn't bother to control the grin that spread over his face.

"Fortunately you made the introductions quickly, Ana," he said. "I like my nose precisely the way it is." He held out a hand. "Nice to meet you. Ana was telling us she had new neighbors."

"He's the one with horses, Daddy."

"I remember." Boone found Sebastian's grip firm and strong. He might have appreciated it if he hadn't seen the gleam of amusement in the man's eyes. "You're recently married?"

"Indeed I am. My..." He turned when the screen door slammed. "Ah, here she is now. Light of my life."

A tall, slim woman with short, tousled hair strode over in dusty boots. "Cut it out, Donovan."

"My blushing bride." It was obvious they were laughing at each other. He took his wife's hand and kissed it. "Ana's neighbors, Boone and Jessie Sawyer. My own true love, Mary Ellen."

"Mel," she corrected quickly. "Donovan's the only one with the nerve to call me Mary Ellen. Great-looking house," she added, with a nod toward the neighboring building.

"I believe Mr. Sawyer writes fairy tales, children's books, much in the manner of Aunt Bryna."

"Oh, yeah? That's cool." Mel smiled down at Jessie. "I bet you like that."

"He writes the best stories in the world. And this is Daisy. We taught her to sit. Can I come see your horses?"

"Sure." Mel crouched down to ruffle the pup's fur. While Mel engaged Jessie in conversation about horses and dogs, Sebastian looked back at Boone.

"It is a lovely house you have," he said. Actually, he'd toyed with buying it himself. Amusement lit his eyes again. "Excellent location."

"We like it." Boone decided it was foolish to pretend not to understand the meaning behind the words. "We like it very much." Very deliberately, he reached out to trail a fingertip down Ana's cheek. "You're looking a little pale this morning, Anastasia."

"I'm fine." It was easy enough to keep her voice even, but she knew very well how simple it would be for Sebastian to see what she was thinking. Already she could feel his gentle probing, and she was quite certain he was poking his nosy mental fingers into Boone's brain. "If you'll excuse me, I promised Sebastian some hawthorn."

"Didn't you pick any last night?"

Her gaze met his, held it. "I have other uses for that."

"We'll get out of your way. Come on, Jess." He reached for his daughter's hand. "Nice meeting both of you. I'll see you soon, Ana."

Sebastian had the tact to wait until Boone was out of earshot. "Well, well ... I go away for a couple of weeks, and look at the trouble you get into."

"Don't be ridiculous." Ana turned her back and started toward an herb bed. "I'm not in any sort of trouble."

"Darling, darling Ana, your friend and neighbor was prepared to rip my throat out until you introduced me as your cousin."

"I'd have protected you," Mel said solemnly.

"My hero."

"Besides," Mel went on, "it looked to me as though he was more in the mood to drag Ana off by the hair than tackle you."

"You're both being absurd." Ana snipped hawthorn without looking up. "He's a very nice man."

"I'm sure," Sebastian murmured. "But, you see, men understand this territorial thing—which is, of course, an obscure concept to the female."

"Oh, please." Mel shoved an elbow in his ribs.

"Facts are facts, my dear Mary Ellen. I had intruded on his territory. Or so he thought. Naturally, I would only think less of him if he had made no effort to defend it."

"Naturally," Mel said dryly.

"Tell me, Ana, just how involved are you?"

"That's none of your business." She straightened, deftly wrapping the stems of the hawthorn. "And I'll thank you to keep out of it, cousin. I know very well you were poking in."

"Which is why you blocked me. Your neighbor wasn't so successful."

"It's rude," she muttered, "unconscionably rude, the way you peek into people's heads at the drop of a hat."

"He likes to show off," Mel said sympathetically.

"Unfair." Disgusted, Sebastian shook his head. "I do not poke or peek at the drop of a hat. I always have an excellent reason. In this case, being your only male relative on the continent, I feel it's my duty to survey the situation, and the players.''

Mel could only roll her eyes as Ana's spine stiffened. ''Really?'' Eyes bright, Ana jammed a finger into Sebastian's chest. ''Then let me set you straight. Just because I'm a woman doesn't mean I need protection or guidance or anything else from a male—relative or otherwise. I've been handling my own life for twenty-six years.''

''Twenty-seven next month,'' Sebastian added helpfully.

''And I can continue to handle it. What's between Boone and me—''

''Ah.'' He held up a triumphant finger. ''So there is something between you.''

''Stuff it, Sebastian.''

''She only talks like that when she paints herself into a corner,'' Sebastian told Mel. ''Usually she's extremely mild and well-mannered.''

''Careful, or I'll give Mel a potion to put in your soup that'll freeze your vocal cords for a week.''

''Oh yeah?'' Intrigued by the idea, Mel tilted her head. ''Can I have it anyway?''

''A lot of good it would do you, since I do all the cooking,'' Sebastian pointed out. Then he scooped Ana up in a hug. ''Come on, darling, don't be angry. I have to worry about you. It's my job.''

''There's nothing to worry about.'' But she was softening.

''Are you in love with him?''

Instantly she stiffened. ''Really, Sebastian, I've only known him for a week.''

''What difference does that make?'' He gave Mel a long look over Ana's head. ''It took me less than that to realize the reason Mel irritated me so much was that I was crazy about her. Of course, it took her longer to understand she was madly in love with me. But she has such a hard head.''

''I'm getting that potion,'' Mel decided.

Ignoring the threat, he drew back to consider Ana at arm's length. ''I ask because he definitely has more than a neighborly interest in you. As a matter of fact, he—''

''That's enough. Whatever you dug out of his head, you keep to yourself. I mean it, Sebastian,'' she said before he could interrupt. ''I prefer doing things my own way.''

''If you insist,'' he said with a sigh.

''I do. Now take your hawthorn and go home and be newlyweds.''

''Now that's the best idea I've heard all day.'' Taking a firm grip on her husband's arm, Mel tugged him back. ''Leave her alone, Donovan. Ana's perfectly capable of handling her own affairs.''

''And if she's going to have one, she should know—''

''Out.'' On a strangled laugh, Ana gave him a shove. ''Out of my yard. I have work to do. If I need a psychic, I'll call you.''

He relented and gave her a kiss. ''See that you do.'' A new smile began to bloom as he walked away with his wife. ''I believe we'll stop by and see Morgana and Nash.''

''That's fine.'' She shot a last glance over her shoulder. ''I'd like to hear what they have to say about this guy myself.''

Sebastian laughed and hugged her close. ''You are a woman after my own heart.''

"No, I'm not." She kissed him soundly. "I've already got it."

For the next several days, Ana busied herself indoors. It wasn't that she was avoiding Boone—at least not to any great extent. She simply had a lot to do. Her medicinal supplies had become sadly depleted. Just that day, she'd had a call from a client in Carmel who was out of the elixir for her rheumatism. Ana had had just enough to ship, but that meant she had to make more as soon as possible. Even now she had dried primrose simmering with motherwort on the stove.

In the little room adjoining the kitchen through a wide archway, she had her distilling flasks, condensers, burners and bottles, along with vials and silver bowls and candles, set up for the day. To the casual eye, the room resembled a small chemistry lab. But there was a marked difference between chemistry and alchemy. In alchemy there was ritual, and the meticulous use of astrological timing.

All of the flowers and roots and herbs she had harvested by moonlight had been carefully washed in morning dew. Others, plucked under different phases of the moon, had already been prepared for their specific uses.

There was syrup of poppy to be distilled, and there was hyssop to be dried for cough syrup. She needed some oil of clary for a specialty perfume, and she could combine that with some chamomile for a digestive aid. There were infusions and decoctions to be completed, as well as both oils and incense.

Plenty to do, Ana thought, particularly since she had the touch of magic from the flowers picked in moonlight. And she enjoyed her work, the scents that filled her kitchen and workroom, the pretty pink leaves of the flowering marjoram, the deep purple of foxglove, the sunny touch of the practical marigold.

They were lovely, and she could never resist setting some in vases or bowls around the house. She was testing a dilution of gentian, grimacing at the bitter taste, when Boone knocked on her screen door.

"I really do need sugar this time," he told her with a quick, charming grin that had her heart pumping fast. "I'm homeroom mother this week, and I have to make three dozen cookies for tomorrow."

Tilting her head, she studied him. "You could buy them."

"What homeroom mother worth her salt serves the first grade class store-bought? A cup would do it."

The image of him baking made her smile. "I probably have one. Come on in. Just let me finish this up."

"It smells fabulous in here." He leaned over to peek into the pots simmering on the stove. "What are you doing?"

"Don't!" She warned, just as he was about to dip a finger in a black glass pan cooling on the counter. "That's belladonna. Not for internal consumption in that form."

"Belladonna." His brows drew together. "You're making poison?"

"I'm making a lotion—an anodyne—for neuralgia, rheumatism. And it isn't a poison if it's brewed and dispensed properly. It's a sedative."

Frowning, he looked into the room behind, with its chemical equipment and its bubbling brews. "Don't you have to have a license or something?"

"I'm a qualified herbal practitioner, with a degree in pharmacognosy, if that relieves you." She batted his hand away from a pot. "And this is not something for the novice."

"Got anything for insomnia—besides belladonna? No offense."

She was instantly concerned. "Are you having trouble sleeping? Are you feverish?" She lifted a hand to his brow, then went still when he took her wrist.

"Yes, to both questions. You could say you're the cause and the cure." He brought her hand from his brow to his lips. "I may be homeroom mother, but I'm still a man, Ana. I can't stop thinking about you." He turned her hand over, pressing those lips to the inside of her wrist, where the pulse was beginning to jerk. "And I can't stop wanting you."

"I'm sorry if I'm giving you restless nights."

His brow quirked. "Are you?"

She couldn't quite suppress the smile. "I'm trying to be. It's hard not to be flattered that thinking about me is keeping you awake. And it's hard to know what to do." She turned away to switch off the heat on the stove. "I've been feeling a little restless myself." Her eyes closed when his hands came down on her shoulders.

"Make love with me." He brushed a kiss on the back of her neck. "I won't hurt you, Ana."

Not purposely, she thought. Never that. There was so much kindness in him. But would they hurt each other if she gave in to what she wanted, needed from him, and held back that part of herself that made her what she was?

"It's a big step for me, Boone."

"For me, too." Gently he turned her to face him. "There's been no one for me since Alice died. In the past couple of years there was a woman or two, but nothing that meant any more than filling a physical emptiness. No one I've wanted to spend time with, to be with, to talk to. I care about you.'' He lowered his mouth to hers, very carefully, very softly. ''I don't know how I came to care this much, this quickly, but I do. I hope you believe that.''

Even without a true link, she couldn't help but feel it. It made things more complicated somehow. ''I do believe you.''

''I've been thinking. Seeing as I haven't been sleeping, I've had plenty of time for it.'' Absently he tapped a loosened pin back into her hair. ''The other night, I was rushing you, probably scared you.''

''No.'' Then she shrugged and turned back to filter one of her mixtures into a bottle, already labeled. ''Yes, actually, I guess you did.''

''If I'd known you were... If I'd realized you'd never...''

With a sigh, she capped the bottle. ''My virginity is by choice, Boone, and nothing I'm uncomfortable with.''

''I didn't mean—'' He let out a hissing breath. ''I'm doing a great job with this.''

She chose another funnel, another bottle, and poured. ''You're nervous.''

With some chagrin, he noted that her hands were rock-steady when she capped the next bottle. ''I think terrified comes closer. I was rough with you, and I shouldn't have been. For a lot of reasons. The fact that you're inexperienced is only one of them.''

''You weren't rough.'' She continued to work to hide her nerves, which were jumping every bit as much as his. As long as she had to concentrate on what she was doing, she could at least pretend to be calm and confident. "You're a passionate man. That's not something to apologize for."

"I'm apologizing for pressuring you. And for coming over here today fully intending to keep things light and easy, and then pressuring you again."

Her lips curved as she walked to the sink to soak her pans. "Is that what you're doing?"

"I told myself I wasn't going to ask you to go to bed with me—even though I want you to. I was going to ask if you'd spend some time with me. Come to dinner, or go out, or whatever people do when they're trying to get to know each other."

"I'd like to come to dinner, or go out, or whatever."

"Good." That hadn't been so hard, he decided. "Maybe this weekend. Friday night. I should be able to find a sitter." His eyes clouded. "Somebody I can trust."

"I thought you were going to cook for me and Jessie."

A weight lifted. "You wouldn't mind?"

"I think I'd enjoy it."

"Okay, then." He framed her face in his hands. "Okay." The kiss was very sweet, and if it felt as if something inside were going to rip in two, he told himself, he could deal with it. "Friday."

It wasn't difficult to smile, even if her system felt as if it had been rocked by a small earthquake. "I'll bring the wine."

"Good." He wanted to kiss her again, but he was afraid he'd scare her off. "I'll see you then."

"Boone." She stopped him before he'd reached the door. "Don't you want your sugar?"

He grinned. "I lied."

Her eyes narrowed. "You're not homeroom mother, and you're not baking cookies?"

"No, that was true. But I have five pounds in the pantry. Hey, it worked." He was whistling as he walked out the door.

Chapter Six

"Why isn't Ana here yet? When is she coming?"

"Soon," Boone answered for the tenth time. Too soon, he was afraid. He was behind in everything. The kitchen was a disaster. He'd used too many pans. Then again, he always did. He could never figure out how anyone cooked without using every pot, pan and bowl available.

The chicken cacciatore smelled pretty good, but he was uncertain of the results. Stupid, he supposed, absolutely stupid to try out a new recipe at such a time, but he'd figured Ana was worth more than their usual Friday-night meatloaf.

Jessie was driving him crazy, which was a rarity. She was overexcited at the thought of having Ana over, and she'd been pestering him without pause ever since he'd brought her home from school.

The dog had chosen that afternoon to chew up Boone's bed pillows, so he'd spent a great deal of valuable time chasing dog and feathers. The washing machine had overflowed, flooding the laundry room. He was much too male to consider calling a repairman, so he'd torn the machine apart and put it back together again.

He was pretty sure he'd fixed it.

His agent had called to tell him that *A Third Wish for Miranda* had been optioned for an animated feature by one of the major studios. That would have been good news at any other time, but now he was expected to fit a trip to L.A. into his schedule.

Jessie had decided she wanted to be a Brownie and had generously volunteered him as a Brownie leader.

The thought of having a group of six- and seven-year-old girls looking to him to teach them how to make jewelry boxes out of egg cartons chilled his blood.

With a lot of ingenuity and plenty of cowardice, he thought, he might be able to ease his way out of it.

"Are you sure she's coming, Daddy? Are you sure?"

"Jessica." The warning note in his voice was enough to make her lower lip poke out. "Do you know what happens to little girls who keep asking the same question?"

"Nuh-uh."

"Keep it up and you'll find out. Go make sure Daisy's not eating the furniture."

"Are you awfully mad at Daisy?"

"Yes. Now go on or you're next." He softened the order with a gentle pat on her bottom. "Beat it, brat, or I'll put you in the pot and have you for dinner."

Two minutes later, he heard the mayhem that meant Jessie had located Daisy, and girl and dog were now wrestling. The high-pitched yelps and happy squeals played hell with the headache pulsing behind his eyes.

Just need an aspirin, he thought, an hour or two of quiet, and a vacation on Maui.

He was on the point of giving a roar that would probably pop his head off his shoulders when Ana knocked.

"Hi. Smells good."

He hoped it did. She looked much better than good. He hadn't seen her in a dress before, and the swirl of watercolor silk did wonderful things for her slim body. Things like showing off those soft white shoulders under thin straps. With it she wore an amulet on a long chain that had the square of engraved gold hanging just below her breasts. Crystals glinted in it, drawing the eye, and were echoed by the tear-shaped drops at her ears.

She smiled. "You did say Friday."

"Yeah. Friday."

"Then are you going to ask me in?"

"Sorry." Lord, he felt like a bumbling teenager. No, he decided as he slid the screen open for her, no teenager had ever been this bumbling. "I'm a little distracted."

Ana's brows lifted as she surveyed the chaos of pots and bowls. "So I see. Would you like some help?"

"I think I've got it under control." He took the bottle she offered, noting that the pale green bottle was etched with symbols and that it carried no label. "Homemade?"

"Yes, my father makes it. He has..." Her eyes lit with secrets and humor. "...A magic touch."

"Brewed in the dungeons of Castle Donovan."

"As a matter of fact, yes." She left it at that, and wandered to the stove as he took out some glasses. "No Bugs Bunny this time?"

"I'm afraid Bugs met a fatal accident in the dishwasher." He poured the clear golden wine into the crystal glasses. "It wasn't pretty."

She laughed and lifted her glass in a toast. "To neighbors."

"To neighbors," he agreed, clinking crystal against crystal. "If they all looked like you, I'd be a dead man." He sipped, then lifted a brow. "Next time we'll have to drink to your father. This is incredible."

"One of his many hobbies, you might say."

"What's in it?"

"Apples, honeysuckle, starlight. You can give him your compliments, if you like. He and the rest of my family should be here for All Hallows' Eve. Halloween."

"I know what it is. Jessie's torn between being a fairy princess or a rock star. Your parents travel all the way to the States for Halloween?"

"Usually. It's a kind of family tradition." Unable to resist, she took the lid off the pan and sniffed. "Well, well, I'm impressed."

"That was the idea." Equally unable to resist, he lifted a handful of her hair. "You know that story I told you the day Daisy knocked you down? I find myself compelled to write it. So much so that I've put what I was working on aside."

"It was a lovely story."

"Normally I could have made it wait. But I need to know why the woman was bound inside the castle all those years. Was it a spell, one of her own making?

What was the enchantment that made the man climb the wall to find her?''

"That's for you to decide."

"No, that's for me to find out."

"Boone..." She lifted a hand to his, then looked down quickly. "What have you done to yourself?"

"Just rapped my knuckles." He flexed his fingers and shrugged. "Fixing the washing machine."

"You should have come over and let me tend to this." She ran her fingers over the scraped skin, wishing she was in a position to heal it. "It's painful."

He started to deny it, then realized his mistake. "I always kiss Jessie's hurts to make them better."

"A kiss works wonders," she agreed, and obliged him by touching her lips to the wound. Briefly, very briefly, she risked a link to be certain there was no real pain and no chance of infection. She found that, while the knuckles were merely sore, he did have real pain from a tension headache working behind his eyes. That, at least, she could help him with.

With a smile, she brushed the hair from his brow. "You've been working too hard, getting the house in order, writing your story, worrying if you made the right decision to move Jessie."

"I didn't realize I was that transparent."

"It isn't so difficult to see." She laid her fingers on either side of his temples, massaging in small circles. "Now you've gone to all this trouble to cook me dinner."

"I wanted—"

"I know." She held steady as she felt the pain flash behind her own eyes. To distract him, she touched her lips to his as she absorbed the ache and let it slowly fade. "Thank you."

"You're very welcome," he murmured, and deepened the kiss.

Her hands slid away from his temples, lay weakly on his shoulders. It was much more difficult to absorb this ache—this ache that spread so insidiously through her. Pulsing, throbbing. Tempting.

Much too tempting.

"Boone." Wary, she slipped out of his arms. "We're rushing this."

"I told you I wouldn't. That's not going to stop me from kissing you whenever I get the chance." He picked up his wine, then hers, offering her glass to her again. "Nothing goes beyond that until you say so."

"I don't know whether to thank you for that or not. I know I should."

"No. There's no more need to thank me for that than there is to thank me for wanting you. It's just the way it is. Sometimes I think about Jessie growing up. It gives me some bad moments. And I know that if there was any man who pushed or pressured her into doing what she wasn't ready to do I'd just have to kill him." He sipped, and grinned. "And, of course, if she thinks she's going to be ready to do anything of the kind before she's, say, forty, I'll just lock her in her room until the feeling passes."

It made her laugh, and she realized as he stood there, with his back to the cluttered, splattered stove, a dishcloth hanging from the waist of his slacks, that she was very, very close to falling in love with him.

Once she had, she would be ready. And nothing would make the feeling pass.

"Spoken like a true paranoid father."

"Paranoia and fatherhood are synonymous. Take my word for it. Wait until Nash has those twins. He'll start thinking about health insurance and dental hygiene. A sneeze in the middle of the night will send him into a panic.''

''Morgana will keep him level. A paranoid father only needs a sensible mother to...'' Her words trailed off as she cursed herself. ''I'm sorry.''

''It's all right. It's easier when people don't feel they have to tiptoe around it. Alice has been gone for four years. Wounds heal, especially if you have good memories.'' There was a thud from the next room, and the sound of racing feet. ''And a six-year-old who keeps you on your toes.''

At that moment, Jessie ran in and threw herself at Ana.

''You came! I thought you'd never get here.''

''Of course I came. I never turn down a dinner invitation from my favorite neighbors.''

As Boone watched them, he realized his headache had vanished. Odd, he thought as he switched off the stove and prepared to serve dinner. He'd never gotten around to taking an aspirin.

It wasn't what he would call a quiet, romantic dinner. He had lit candles and clipped flowers in the garden he'd inherited when he'd bought the house. They had the meal in the dining alcove, with its wide, curved window, with music from the sea and birdsong. A perfect setting for romance.

But there were no murmured secrets or whispered promises. Instead, there was laughter and a child's bubbling voice. The talk was not about what the candlelight did to her skin, or how it deepened the pure gray of her eyes. It centered on first grade, on what

Daisy had done that day and on the fairy tale still brewing in Boone's mind.

When dinner was over, and Ana had listened to Jessie's exploits at school, along with those of Jessie's new and very best friend, Lydia, she announced that she and the child were assuming kitchen duty.

"No, I'll take care of it later." He was very comfortable in the sunset-washed dining alcove, and he remembered too vividly the mess he'd left behind in the kitchen. "Dirty dishes don't go anywhere."

"You cooked." Ana was already rising to stack the dishes. "When my father cooks, my mother washes up. And vice versa. Donovan rules. Besides, the kitchen's a good place for girl talk, isn't it, Jessie?"

Jessie didn't have any idea, but she was instantly intrigued by the notion. "I can help. I hardly ever break any dishes."

"And men aren't allowed in the kitchen during girl talk." She leaned conspiratorially toward Jessie. "Because they just get in the way." She sent Boone an arch look. "I think you and Daisy could use a walk on the beach."

"I don't..." A walk on the beach. Alone. With no KP. "Really?"

"Really. Take your time. Jessie, when I was in town the other day, I saw the cutest dress. It was blue, just the color of your eyes, and had a big satin bow." Ana stopped, a pile of dishes in her hands, and stared at Boone. "Still here?"

"Just leaving."

As he walked out in the deepening twilight with Daisy romping around him, he could hear the light music of female laughter coming through his windows.

"Daddy said you were born in a castle," Jessie said as she helped Ana load the dishwasher.

"That's right. In Ireland."

"A for-real castle?"

"A real castle, near the sea. It has towers and turrets, secret passageways, and a drawbridge."

"Just like in Daddy's books."

"Very much like. It's a magic palace." Ana listened to the sound of water as she rinsed dishes and thought of the squabbles and laughing voices in that huge kitchen, with a fire going in the hearth and the good, yeasty smell of fresh bread perfuming the air. "My father and his brothers were born there, and his father, and his, and further back than I can say."

"If I were born in a castle, I would always live there." Jessie stood close to Ana while they worked, enjoying without knowing why, the scent of woman, and the lighter timbre of a female voice. "Why did you move away?"

"Oh, it's still home, but sometimes you have to move away, to make your own place. Your own magic."

"Like Daddy and me did."

"Yes." She closed the dishwasher and began to fill the sink with hot, soapy water for the pots and pans. "You like living here in Monterey?"

"I like it a lot. Nana said I might get homesick when the novelty wears off. What's novelty?"

"The newness." Not a very wise thing to suggest to an impressionable child, Ana mused. But she imagined Nana's nose was out of joint. "If you do get homesick, you should try to remember that the very best place to be is usually where you are."

"I like where Daddy is, even if he took me to Timbuktu."

"Excuse me?"

"Grandma Sawyer said he might as well have moved us to Timbuktu." Jessie accepted the clean pot Ana handed her and began to dry, an expression of deep concentration on her face. "Is that a real place?"

"Um-hmm. But it's also a kind of expression that means far away. Your grandparents are missing you, sunshine. That's all."

"I miss them, too, but I get to talk to them on the phone, and Daddy helped me type a letter on his computer. Do you think you could marry Daddy so Grandma Sawyer would get off his back?"

The pan Ana had been washing plopped into the suds and sent a small tidal wave over the lip of the sink. "I don't think so."

"I heard him telling Grandma Sawyer that she was on his back all the time to find a wife so he wouldn't be lonely and I wouldn't have to grow up without a mother. His voice had that mad sound in it he gets when I do something really wrong, or like when Daisy chewed up his pillow. And he said he'd be damned if he'd tie himself down just to keep the peace."

"I see." Ana pressed her lips hard together to keep the proper seriousness on her face. "I don't think he'd like you to repeat it, Jessie, especially in those words."

"Do you think Daddy's lonely?"

"No. No, I don't. I think he's very happy with you, and with Daisy. If he decided to get married one day, it would be because he found somebody all of you loved very much."

"I love you."

"Oh, sunshine." Soapy hands and all, Ana scooted down to give Jessie a hug and a kiss. "I love you, too."

"Do you love Daddy?"

I wish I knew. "It's different," she said. She knew she was navigating on boggy ground. "When you grow up, love means different things. But I'm very happy that you moved here and we can all be friends."

"Daddy never had a lady over to dinner before."

"Well, you've only been here a couple of weeks."

"I mean ever, at all. Not in Indiana, either. So I thought maybe it meant that you were going to get married and live with us here so Grandma Sawyer would get off his back and I wouldn't be a poor motherless child."

"No." Ana did her best to disguise a chuckle. "It meant that we like each other and wanted to have dinner." She checked the window to make certain Boone wasn't on his way back. "Does he always cook like this?"

"He always makes a really big mess, and sometimes he says those words—you know?"

"I know."

"He says them when he has to clean it up. And today he was in a really bad mood 'cause Daisy ate his pillow and there were feathers all over and the washing machine exploded and he maybe has to go on a business trip."

"That's a lot for one day." She bit her lip. Really, she didn't want to pump the child, but she was curious. "He's going to take a trip?"

"Maybe to the place where they make movies, 'cause they want to make one out of his book."

"That's wonderful."

"He has to think about it. That's what he says when he doesn't want to say yes but probably he's going to."

This time Ana didn't bother to smother the chuckle. "You certainly have his number."

By the time they'd finished the kitchen, Jessie was yawning. "Will you come up and see my room? I put everything away like Daddy said to when we have company."

"I'd love to see your room."

The packing boxes were gone, Ana noted as they moved from the kitchen into the high-ceilinged living room, with its open balcony and curving stairs. The furniture there looked comfortably lived-in, bold, bright colors in fabrics that appeared tough enough to stand up under the hands and feet of an active child.

It could have used some flowers at the window, she mused. Some scented candles in brass holders on the mantel. Perhaps a few big, plump pillows scattered here and there. Still, there were homey family touches in the framed photographs, the ticking grandfather clock. And clever, whimsical ones, like the brass dragon's-head andirons standing guard on the stone hearth, and the unicorn rocking horse in the corner.

And if there was a little dust on the banister, that only added to the charm.

"I got to pick out my own bed," Jessie was telling her. "And once everything settles down I can pick out wallpaper if I want to. That's where Daddy sleeps." She pointed to the right, and Ana had a glimpse of a big bed under a jade-colored quilt—sans pillows—a handsome old chest of drawers with a missing pull, and a few stray feathers.

"He has his own bathroom in there, too, with a big tub that has jets and a shower that's all glass and has water coming out of both sides. I get to use the one out here, and it has two sinks and this little thing that isn't a toilet but looks like one."

"A bidet?"

"I guess so. Daddy says it's fancy and mostly for ladies. This is my room."

It was a little girl's fantasy, one provided by a man who obviously understood that childhood was all too short and very precious. All pink and white, the canopy bed sat in the center, a focal point surrounded by shelves of dolls and books and bright toys, a snowy dresser with a curvy mirror, and a child-sized desk littered with colored paper and crayons.

On the walls were lovely framed illustrations from fairy tales. Cinderella rushing down the steps of a silvery castle, a single glass slipper left behind. Rapunzel, her golden hair spilling out of a high tower window while she looked longingly down at her prince. The sly, endearing elf from one of Boone's books, and—a complete surprise to Ana—one of her aunt's prized illustrations.

"This is from *The Golden Ball*."

"The lady who wrote it sent it to Daddy for me when I was just little. Next to Daddy's I like her stories best."

"I had no idea," Ana murmured. As far as she'd known, her aunt had never parted with one of her drawings except to family.

"Daddy did the elf," Jessie pointed out. "All the rest my mother did."

"They're beautiful." Not just skillful, Ana thought, and perhaps not as clever as Boone's elf or as elegant as her aunt's drawing, but lovely, and as true to the spirit of a fairy tale as magic itself.

"She drew them just for me, when I was a baby. Nana said Daddy should put them away so they wouldn't make me sad. But they don't. I like to look at them."

"You're very lucky to have something so beautiful to remember her by."

Jessie rubbed her sleepy eyes and struggled to hold back a yawn. "I have dolls, too, but I don't play with them much. My grandmothers like to give them to me, but I like the stuffed walrus my daddy got me better. Do you like my room?"

"It's lovely, Jessie."

"I can see the water, and your yard, from the windows." She tucked back the billowing sheer curtains to show off her view. "And that's Daisy's bed, but she likes to sleep with me." Jessie pointed out the wicker dog bed, with its pink cushion.

"Maybe you'd like to lie down until Daisy comes back."

"Maybe." Jessie sent Ana a doubtful look. "But I'm not really tired. Do you know any stories?"

"I could probably think of one." She picked Jessie up to sit her on the bed. "What kind would you like?"

"A magic one."

"The very best kind." She thought for a moment, then smiled. "Ireland is an old country," she began, slipping an arm around the girl. "And it's filled with secret places, dark hills and green fields, water so blue it hurts the eyes to stare at it for long. There's been magic there for so many centuries, and it's still a safe place for faeries and elves and witches."

"Good witches or bad ones?"

"Both, but there's always been more good than bad, not only in witches, but in everything."

"Good witches are pretty," Jessie said, stroking a hand down Ana's arm. "That's how you know. Is this a story about a good witch?"

"It is indeed. A very good and very beautiful witch. And a very good and very handsome one, too."

"Men aren't witches," Jessie informed her, giggling. "They're wizards."

"Who's telling the story?" Ana kissed the top of Jessie's head. "Now, one day, not so many years ago, a beautiful young witch traveled with her two sisters to visit their old grandfather. He was a very powerful witch—wizard—but had grown cranky and bored in his old age. Not far from the manor where he lived was a castle. And there lived three brothers. They were triplets, and very powerful wizards, as well. For as long as anyone could remember, the old wizard and the family of the three brothers had carried on a feud. No one remembered the why of it any longer, but the feud ran on, as they tend to do. So the families spoke not a word to each other for an entire generation."

Ana shifted Jessie to her lap, stroking the child's hair as she told the story. She was smiling to herself, unaware that she'd lapsed into her native brogue.

"But the young witch was headstrong, as well as beautiful. And her curiosity was great. And on a fine day in high summer, she slipped out of the manor house and walked through the fields and the meadows toward the castle of her grandfather's enemy. Along the way was a pond, and she paused there to dangle her bare feet in the water and study the castle in the distance. And while she sat, with her feet wet and her hair down around her shoulders, a frog plopped up on the bank and spoke to her.

"'Fair lady,' he said, 'why do you wander on my land?'

"Well, the young witch was not at all surprised to hear a frog speak. After all, she knew too much of magic, and she sensed a trick. 'Your land?' she said. 'Frogs have only the water, and the marsh. I walk where I choose.'

"'But your feet are in my water. So you must pay a forfeit.'

"So she laughed and told him that she owed a common frog nothing at all.

"Well, needless to say, the frog was puzzled by her attitude. After all, it wasn't every day he plopped down and spoke to a beautiful woman, and he had expected at least a shriek or some fearful respect. He was quite fond of playing tricks, and was sorely disappointed that this one wasn't working as he'd hoped. He explained that he was no ordinary frog, and if she didn't agree to pay the forfeit he would have to punish her. And what forfeit did he expect? His answer was a kiss, which was no more and no less than she had expected, for as I said, she was young, but not foolish.

"She said that she doubted very much if he would turn into a handsome prince if she did so, and that she would save her kisses.

"Now the frog was very frustrated, and he plied more magic, whistling up the wind, shaking the leaves in the trees, but she merely yawned at this. At the end of his tether, the frog jumped right into her lap and began to berate her. To teach him a lesson for his forwardness, she plucked him up and tossed him into the water. When he surfaced, he wasn't a frog at all, but a young man, quite wet and furious to have had his joke turned on him. After he swam to shore, they stood on the bank and shouted at each other, threatening spells and curses, sending lightning walking the sky, and shooting the air with thunder. Though she threatened him with the hounds of hell and worse, he said he would have his forfeit regardless, for it was his land, his water, and his right. So he kissed her soundly.

"And it took only that to turn the heat in her heart to warmth, and the fury in his breast to love. For even witches can fall under that most powerful of spells. There and then they pledged to each other, marrying within the month right there on the banks on the pond. And they were happy, then and after, with lives full of love. Still, every year, on a day in high summer, though she is no longer young, she goes to the pond, dangles her feet and waits for an indignant frog to join her."

Ana lifted the sleeping girl. She had told the end of the story only for herself—or so she thought. But as she drew back the cover, Boone's hand closed over hers.

"That was a pretty good story for an amateur. Must be the Irish."

"It's an old family one," she said, thinking how often she had heard how her mother and father had met.

He expertly unlaced his daughter's shoes. "Be careful. I might steal it from you."

As he tucked the covers around Jessie, Daisy took a running leap and landed on the foot of the bed. "Did you enjoy your walk?"

"After I stopped feeling guilty for leaving you with the dishes—which took about ninety seconds." He brushed Jessie's hair from her brow and bent to kiss her good-night. "One of the most enviable things about childhood is being able to drop off to sleep like that."

"Are you still having trouble?"

"I've got a lot on my mind." Taking Ana's hand, he drew her out of the room, leaving the door open, as he always did. "A lot of it's you, but there are a few other things."

"Honest, but not flattering." She paused at the top of the stairs. "Seriously, Boone, I could give you something—" She flushed and chuckled when she saw the light come into his eyes. "A very mild, very safe herbal remedy."

"I'd rather have sex."

Shaking her head, she continued downstairs. "You don't take me seriously."

"On the contrary."

"I mean as an herbalist."

"I don't know anything about that sort of thing, but I don't discount it." He wasn't about to let her dose him, either. "Why'd you get into it?"

"It's always been an interest. There have been healers in my family for generations."

"Doctors?"

"Not exactly."

Boone picked up the wine and two glasses as they walked through the kitchen and out onto the deck. "You didn't want to be a doctor."

"I didn't feel qualified to go into medicine."

"Now that's a very odd thing for a modern, independent woman to say."

"One has nothing to do with the other." She accepted the glass he offered. "It's not possible to heal everyone. And I . . . have difficulty being around suffering. What I do is my way of satisfying my needs and protecting myself." It was the most she felt she could give him. "And I like working alone."

"I know the feeling. Both my parents thought I was crazy. The writing was okay, but they figured I'd write the great American novel, at the very least. Fairy tales were hard for them to swallow at first."

"They must be proud of you."

"In their way. They're nice people," he said slowly, realizing he'd never discussed them with anyone but Alice. "They've always loved me. God knows they dote on Jessie. But they have a hard time understanding that I might not want what they want. A house in the suburbs, a decent golf game, and a spouse who's devoted to me."

"None of those things are bad."

"No, and I had it once—except for the golf game. I'd rather not spend the rest of my life convincing them that I'm content with the way things are now." He twined a lock of her hair around his fingers. "Don't you get the same sort of business from yours? Anastasia, when are you going to settle down with some nice young man and raise a family?"

"No." She laughed into her wine. "Absolutely not." The very idea of her mother or father saying, even thinking, such a thing made her laugh again. "I suppose you could say my parents are...eccentric." Comfortable, she laid her head back and looked at the stars. "I think they'd both be appalled if I settled for nice. You didn't tell me you had one of Aunt Bryna's illustrations."

"When you made the family connection, you were ready to chew me up and spit me out. It didn't seem appropriate. Then, I guess, it slipped my mind."

"Obviously she thinks highly of you. She only gave one to Nash after the wedding, and he'd been coveting one for years."

"That so? I'll be sure to rub his nose in it the next time I see him." Tipping up her chin with a finger, he turned her face toward his. "It's been a long time since I sat on a porch and necked. I'm wondering if I still have the hang of it."

He brushed his lips over hers, once, twice, a third time, until hers trembled open in invitation. He took the glass from her fingers, set it aside with his as his mouth moved to accept what was offered.

Sweet, so sweet, the taste of her, warming him, soothing him, exciting him. Soft, so soft, the feel of her, tempting him, luring him, charming him. And quiet, so quiet, that quick, catching sigh that sent a streak of lightning zipping up his spine.

But he was no sweaty, fumbling boy groping in the dark. The volcano of needs simmering inside him could be controlled. If he couldn't give her the fullness of his passion, then he could give her the benefit of his experience.

While he filled himself with her, slowly, degree by painful degree, he gave back a care and a tenderness that had her teetering helplessly on that final brink before love.

To be held like this, she thought dimly, with such compassion mixed with the hunger. In all of her imaginings, she had never reached for this. His tongue danced over hers, bringing her all those dark and dusky male flavors. His hands stroked persuasively while the muscles in his arms went taut. When his mouth left hers to cruise down her jaw and over her throat, she arched back, willing, desperately willing, for him to show her more.

It was surrender he felt from her, as clearly as he felt the night breeze against his skin. Knowing it would drive him nearer to the brink, he gave in to the fevered need to touch.

She was small, gloriously soft. Her heart beat frantically under his hand. He could almost taste it, taste that hot satin skin on his lips, on his tongue, deep within his mouth. It was torture not to sample it now, not to drag her dress down to her waist and feast.

The feel of her hardened nipples pressed against the silk had him groaning as he brought his mouth back to hers.

Her mouth was as avid, as desperate. Her hands moved over him as urgently as his over her. She knew, as she gave herself fully to this one moment, that there would be no turning back. They would not love now. It couldn't be now, on the starlit deck, beneath windows where a child might wake and look for her father in the night.

But there was no turning back from being in love. Not for her. She could not change that tidal wave of feeling any more than she could change the blood that coursed through her veins.

And because of it there would come a time, very soon, when she would give to him what she had given to no other.

Overwhelmed, she turned her head, burying her face in his shoulder. ''You have no idea what you do to me.''

''Then tell me.'' He caught the lobe of her ear between his teeth, making her shudder. ''I want to hear you tell me.''

"You make me ache. And yearn." And hope, she thought, squeezing her eyes shut. "No one else has." With a long, shuddering sigh, she drew away. "That's what we're both afraid of."

"I can't deny that." His eyes were like cobalt in the dim light. "And I can't deny that the idea of carrying you upstairs now, taking you into my bed, is something I want as much as I want to go on breathing."

The image had her heart thundering. "Do you believe in the inevitable, Boone?"

"I've had to."

She nodded. "So do I. I believe in destiny, the whims of fate, the tricks of what men used to call the gods. When I look at you, I see the inevitable." She rose, pressed a hand to his shoulder to prevent him from standing with her. "Can you accept that I have secrets I can't tell you, parts of myself I won't share?" She saw both puzzlement and denial in his eyes, and shook her head before he could speak. "Don't answer now.... You need to think it through and be sure. Just as I do."

She leaned down to kiss him, and linked quickly, firmly. She felt his jerk of surprise before she backed away. "Sleep well tonight," she said, knowing that he would now. And that she would not.

Chapter Seven

The one gift Ana always gave herself on her birthday was a completely free day. She could be as lazy as she chose, or as industrious. She could get up at dawn and gorge on ice cream for breakfast, or she could laze in bed until noon watching old movies on television.

The single best plan for the one day of the year that belonged only to her was no plan at all.

She did rise early, indulging herself in a long bath scented with her favorite oils and a muslin bag filled with dried herbs chosen for their relaxing properties. To pamper herself, she mixed up a toning face pack of elder flowers, yogurt and kaolin powder, lounging in the tub with harp music and iced juice while it worked its magic.

With her face tingling and her hair silky from its chamomile shampoo, she slicked on her personalized body oil and slipped into a silk robe the color of moonbeams.

As she walked back into the bedroom, she considered crawling back into bed and dozing to complete the morning's indulgence. But in the center of the room, where there had been nothing but an antique prayer rug when she'd gone in to bathe, stood a large wooden chest.

On a quick cry of pleasure, she dashed over to run her hands over the old carved wood which had been polished to a mirror gleam. It smelled of beeswax and rosemary and felt like silk under her fingers.

It was old, ages old, for it was something she had admired even as a child living in Donovan Castle. A wizard's chest, it was reputed to have resided once in Camelot, commissioned for Merlin by the young Arthur.

With a laughing sigh, she sat back on her heels. They always managed to surprise her, Ana thought. Her parents, her aunts and uncles . . . so far away, but never out of her heart.

The combined power of six witches had sent the chest from Ireland, winking through the air, through time, through space, by means that were less, and more, than conventional.

Slowly she lifted the lid, and the scent of old visions, ancient spells, endless charms, rose out to her. The fragrance was dry, aromatic as crusted petals ground to dust, tangy with the smoke of the cold fire a sorcerer calls in the night.

She knelt, lifting her arms out, the silk sliding down to her elbows as she cupped her hands, palms facing.

Here was power, to be respected, accepted. The words she spoke were in the old tongue, the language of the Wise Ones. The wind she called whipped the curtains, sent her hair flying around her face. The air sang, a thousand harp strings crying in the breeze, then was silent.

Lowering her arms, Ana reached into the chest. A bloodstone amulet, the inner red of the stone bleeding through the deep green, had her sitting back on her heels once more. She knew it had belonged to her mother's family for generations, a healing stone of enormous worth and mighty power. Tears stung the backs of her eyes when she realized that it was being passed to her, as it was only every half century, to denote her as a healer of the highest order.

Her gift, she thought, running her fingers over a stone smoothed by other fingers in other times. Her legacy.

She gently set it back in the chest and reached for the next gift. She lifted out a globe of chalcedony, its almost transparent surface offering her a glimpse of the universe if she should choose to look. This from Sebastian's parents, she knew, for she felt them as she cupped the globe in her hands. Next was a sheepskin, inscribed with the writing of the old tongue. A faery story, she noted as she read and smiled. As old as time, as sweet as tomorrow. Aunt Bryna and Uncle Matthew, she thought as she laid it back inside.

Though the amulet had been from her mother, Ana knew there would always be something special from her father, as well. She found it, and she laughed as she took it out. A frog, as small as her thumbnail, intricately carved in jade.

"Looks just like you, Da," she said, and laughed again. Replacing it, she closed the chest, then rose. It would be afternoon in Ireland, she mused, and there were six people who would be expecting a call to see if she'd enjoyed her gifts.

As she started toward the phone, she heard the knock at her back door. Her heart gave one quick, unsteady leap, then settled calmly. Ireland would have to wait.

Boone held the gift behind his back. There was another package at home, one that he and Jessie had chosen together. But he'd wanted to give Ana this one himself. Alone.

He heard her coming and grinned, the greeting on the tip of his tongue. He was lucky he didn't swallow his tongue, as well as the words, when he saw her.

She was glowing, her hair a rain of pale gold down the back of a robe of silver. Her eyes seemed darker, deeper. How could they be as clear as lake water, he wondered, yet seem to hold a thousand secrets? The gloriously female scent that swirled around her nearly brought him to his knees.

When Quigley rushed against his legs in greeting, Boone jolted as if he'd been shot.

"Boone." With a quiet laugh bubbling in her throat, Ana put her hand on the screen. "Are you all right?"

"Yeah, yeah. I . . . Did I get you up?"

"No." As calm as he was rattled, she opened the door in invitation. "I've been up quite a while. I'm just being lazy." When he continued to stand on the porch, she tilted her head. "Don't you want to come in?"

"Sure." He stepped inside, but kept a careful distance.

He'd been as restrained as could be over the past couple of weeks, resisting the temptation to be alone with her too often, keeping the mood light when they were alone. He realized now that his control had been as much for his sake as for hers.

She was painful to resist, even when they were standing outside in the sunlight, discussing Jessie or gardening, his work or hers.

But this, standing with her, the house empty and silent around them, the mysterious perfume of a woman's art tormenting his senses, was almost too much to bear.

"Is something wrong?" she asked, but she was smiling, as if she knew.

"No, nothing . . . Ah, how are you?"

"I'm fine." Her smile widened, softened. "And you?"

"Great." He thought that if he were any more tense he'd turn to stone. "Fine."

"I was going to make some tea. I'm sorry I don't have any coffee, but perhaps you'd like to join me."

"Tea." He let out a quiet breath. "Terrific." He watched her walk to the stove, the cat winding around her legs like gray rope. She put the kettle on, then poured Quigley's breakfast into his bowl. Crouching down, she stroked the cat as he ate. The robe slipped back like water, exposing one creamy leg.

"How's the woodruff coming, and the hyssop?"

"Ah . . ."

She tossed her hair back as she looked up and smiled. "The herbs I gave you to transplant into your yard."

"Oh, those. They look great."

"I have some basil and some thyme potted in the greenhouse. You might want to take them along, leave them on a windowsill for a while. For cooking." She rose when the kettle began to sputter. "I think you'll find them better than store-bought."

"That'd be great." He was almost relaxed again, he thought. Hoped. It was soothing to watch her brew tea, heating the little china pot, spooning aromatic leaves out of a pale blue jar. He hadn't known a woman could be restful and seductive all at once. "Jessie's been watching those marigold seeds you gave her to plant like a hen watches an egg."

"Just don't let her overwater." Setting the tea to steep, she turned. "Well?"

He blinked. "Well?"

"Boone, are you going to show me what's behind your back or not?"

"Can't fool you, can I?" He held out a box wrapped in bright blue paper. "Happy birthday."

"How did you know it was my birthday?"

"Nash told me. Aren't you going to open it?"

"I certainly am." She tore the paper, revealing a box with the logo of Morgana's shop imprinted on the lid. "Excellent choice," she said. "You couldn't possibly go wrong buying me something from Wicca." She lifted the lid and, with a quiet sigh, drew out a delicate statue of a sorceress carved in amber.

Her head was thrown back and exquisite tendrils of the dark gold hair tumbled down her cloak. Slender arms were raised, bent at the elbows, palms cupped and facing—mirroring the age-old position Ana had assumed over the chest that morning. In one elegant hand she held a small gleaming pearl, in the other a slender silver wand.

"She's beautiful," Ana murmured. "Absolutely beautiful."

"I stopped by the shop last week, and Morgana had just gotten it in. It reminded me of you."

"Thank you." Still holding the statue, she lifted her free hand to his cheek. "You couldn't have found anything more perfect."

She leaned in, rising on her toes to touch her lips to his. She knew exactly what she was doing, just as she knew even as he returned the kiss that he was holding himself on a choke chain of control. Power, as fresh and cool as rainwater, washed into her.

This was what she had been waiting for, this was why she had spent the morning in that ancient female ritual of oils and creams and perfumes.

For him. For her. For their first time together.

There were knots of thorny vines ripping through his stomach, an anvil of need ringing frantically in his head. Though their lips were barely touching, her taste was drugging him, making ideas like restraint and control vague, unimportant concepts. He tried to draw back, but her arms wound silkily around him.

"Ana..."

"Shh." She soothed and excited as her mouth played softly over his. "Just kiss me."

How could he not, when her lips were parting so softly beneath his? He brought his hands to her face, framing it with tensed fingers while he fought a vicious internal war to keep the embrace from going too far.

When the phone rang, he let out a groan that was both frustration and relief. "I'd better go."

"No." She wanted to laugh, but only smiled as she drew out of his arms. Never had she sampled a power more delicious than this. "Please stay. Why don't you pour the tea while I answer that?"

Pour tea, he thought. He'd be lucky if he could lift the pot. System jumbled, he turned blindly to the stove as she took the receiver from the wall phone.

"Mama!" Now she did laugh, and Boone heard the pure joy of it. "Thank you. Thank all of you. Yes, I got it this morning. A wonderful surprise." She laughed again, listening. "Of course. Yes, I'm fine. I'm wonderful. I— Da." She chuckled when her father broke in on the line. "Yes, I know what the frog means. I love it. I love you, too. No, I much prefer it to a real one, thank you." She smiled at Boone when he offered her a cup of tea. "Aunt Bryna? It was a lovely story. Yes, I am. Morgana's very well, so are the twins. Not very much longer now. Yes, you'll be here in time."

Restless, Boone wandered the room, sipping the tea, which was surprisingly good. He wondered what the devil she'd put into it. What the devil she'd put into him. Just listening to her voice was making him ache.

He could handle it, he reminded himself. They'd have a very civilized cup of tea—while he kept his hands off her. Then he'd escape, bury himself in his work for the rest of the day to keep his mind off her, as well.

His story line was all but finished, and he was nearly ready to start on the illustrations. He already knew just what he wanted.

Ana.

With a brisk shake of his head, he gulped more tea. It sounded as if she were going to carry on a conversation with every relative she had. That was fine, that was dandy. It would give him time to calm himself down.

"Yes, I miss you, too. All of you. I'll see you in a couple of weeks. Blessed be."

She was a little teary-eyed when she hung up, but she smiled at Boone. "My family," she explained.

"I gathered."

"They sent me a chest of gifts this morning, and I hadn't gotten a chance to call and thank them."

"That's nice. Look, I really— This morning?" he said with a slight frown. "I didn't see any delivery truck."

"It came early." She looked away to set her cup down. "Special delivery, you could say. They're all looking forward to visiting at the end of the month."

"You'll be glad to see them."

"Always. They were here briefly over the summer, but with all the excitement about Sebastian and Mel getting engaged and married so quickly, there wasn't much time to just be together." She moved to the door to let Quigley out. "Would you like more tea?"

"No, thanks, really. I should go. Get to work." He was edging toward the door himself. "Happy birthday, Ana."

"Boone." She laid a hand on his arm, felt his muscles quiver. "Every year on my birthday I give myself a gift. It's very simple, really. One day to do whatever I choose. Whatever feels right to me." Hardly seeming to move at all, she pulled the door closed and stood between it and him. "I choose you. If you still want me."

Her words seemed to ring in his ears as he stared down at her. She appeared so calm, so utterly serene, she might have been discussing the weather. "You know I want you."

"Yes." She smiled. At that moment she was calm, the eye of the hurricane. "Yes, I do." When she took a step forward, he took one in retreat. Was this seduction? she wondered, keeping her eyes on his. "I see that when I look at you, feel it whenever you touch me. You've been very patient, very kind. You kept your word that nothing would happen between us until I decided it should."

"I'm trying." Unsteady, he took another step back. "It isn't easy."

"Nor for me." She stood where she was, the silver robe shimmering around her in the sunlight. "You've only to accept me, to accept that I'm willing to give you everything I can. Take that, and let it be enough."

"What are you asking me?"

"To be my first," she said simply. "To show me what love can be."

He dared to reach out and touch her hair. "Are you sure?"

"I'm very sure." Offering and asking, she held out both hands. "Will you take me to bed and be my lover?"

How could he answer? There were no words to translate what was churning inside him at that moment. So he wasted no words, only lifted her into his arms.

He carried her as if she were as delicate as the amber enchantress he'd given her. Indeed, he thought of her that way, and he felt a thud of panic at the thought that he wouldn't be careful enough, restrained enough. It was so easy to damage delicacy.

When he reached the base of the stairs and started to climb, his pulse was throbbing in anticipation and fear.

For her sake, he wished it could have been night, a candlelit night filled with soft music and silvery moonglow. Yet somehow it seemed right that he love her, this first time, in the morning, when the sun was growing stronger in a deep blue sky, and music came from the birds that flitted through her garden and the tinkling bells of the wind chimes she had at her windows.

"Where?" he asked her, and she gestured toward her bedroom door.

It smelled of her, a mix of female fragrances and perfumed powders—and something else, something he couldn't quite identify. Like smoke and flowers. The sun streamed gaily through billowing curtains and splashed the huge old bed with the towering carved headboard.

He skirted the trunk, charmed by the rainbow of colors refracted by colored crystals suspended from thin wire in front of each window. Rainbows instead of moonbeams, he thought as he laid her on the bed.

Foolish to be nervous now, she told herself, but her hands trembled lightly when she reached out to hold him against her. She wanted this. Wanted him. Still, the calm certainty she had felt only moments ago had vanished under a wave of nerves and needs.

He could see the need, the nervousness, in her eyes. Could she possible understand that they were a mirror of his? She was so fragile and lovely. Fresh and untouched. His for the taking. And he knew it was vital for them both that he take with tenderness.

"Anastasia." Smothering his own fears, he lifted her hand, pressed his lips to the palm. "I won't hurt you. I swear it."

"I know that." She linked her fingers with his, wishing she could be sure if it was fear of the moment a woman experiences only once in her life, or fear of the overwhelming depth of her love for him, that left her shaky and unsure. "Show me."

With rainbows dancing around them, he lowered his mouth to hers. A deep, drugging kiss that both soothed and enticed. Time spun out, drifted. Stopped. Still there was only his mouth against hers.

He touched her hair, his fingers combing through, tangling in the luxurious length of it. To please himself, he spread it over the pillow, where it lay like a pool of gold dust against soft Irish linen.

When his lips left hers, it was to take a slow, lazy journey of her face until he felt her nervous trembling fall away into pliancy. Even as she surrendered her fears to the light, sweet sensations he brought her, he kept the pace slow, so slow that it seemed they had forever just to kiss.

She heard him murmur to her, reassurances, lovely, lovely promises. The low hum of his voice had her mind floating, her lips curving in a quiet smile as they met his again.

She should have known it would be like this with him. Beautiful, achingly beautiful. He made her feel loved, cherished, safe. When he slipped the robe from her shoulders, she wasn't afraid, but welcomed the feel of his mouth on her flesh. Eager now, she tugged on his shirt, and he hesitated only a moment before helping her remove it.

A groan ripped out of him as his body shuddered. God, the feel of her hands on his bare back. He fought back a wave of greed and kept his own hands easy as he parted her robe.

Her skin was like cream. Unbearably soft and fragrant with oils. It drew him like nectar, inviting him to taste. As he closed his mouth over her breast, the quiet, strangled sound she made deep in her throat echoed like thunder in his head.

Gently he used tongue and lips to take her to that next degree of pleasure, while his own passions licked at him, taunting him, demanding that he hurry, hurry, hurry.

Her eyes were so heavy, impossible to open. How could he know just where to touch, just where to taste, to make her heart shudder in her breast? Yet he did, and her breath sighed out between her lips as he showed her more.

Quiet whispers, a gentle caress. The scent of lavender and fairy roses thickening the air. Smooth sheets growing warm, skin dampening with passion. A rainbow of lights playing against her closed lids.

She floated there, lifted by the magic they made together, her breath quickening a little as he eased her higher, just higher.

Then there was heat, searing, torrid. It erupted inside her so quickly, so violently, that she cried out and struggled against him. "No. No, Boone, I—" Then a flash, a lightning spear of pleasure, that left her limp and dazed and trembling.

"Ana." He had to dig his fisted hands into the mattress to keep from plunging into her, driving them both where he knew the rewards were dark and desperately keen. "Sweet." He kissed her, swallowing her gasping breaths. "So sweet. Don't be afraid."

"No." Rocked to the core, she held him close. His heart was thundering against hers, his body taut as wire. "No. Show me. Show me more."

So he slipped the robe away, driving himself mad with the sight of her naked in a pool of sunlight. Her eyes were open now, dark and steady on his. Beneath the passion just awakened, he saw a trust that humbled him.

He showed her more.

Fears melted away. There was no room for them when her body was vibrating from dozens of more vivid sensations. When he took her to the peak again, she rode out the storm, glorying in the flash of heat, desperate for the next.

He held back, gaining his pleasure from hers, stunned by the way she responded to each touch, to each kiss. Her innocence was his, he knew. With the breath laboring in his lungs, the blood pounding in his head, he entered her, braced for her to stiffen and cry out. Knowing he would have to stop, no matter how his body craved completion, if she asked it of him.

But she didn't stiffen, only gasped out his name as her arms came around him. The brief flash of pain was instantly smothered by a pleasure greater, fuller, than she had ever dreamed possible.

His, she thought. She was his. And she moved against him with an instinct as old as time.

Deeper, he slipped deeper, filling her, rocking her toward that final crest. When she did cry out, her body shuddering, shuddering from the glory of it, he buried his face in her hair and let himself follow.

* * *

He watched the dance of light against the wall, listening to her heart calm and slow. She lay beneath him still, her arms around him, her hands stroking his hair.

He hadn't known it could be like this. That was foolish, he thought. He'd had women before. More, he'd loved before, as deeply as anyone could. Yet this union had been more than he'd ever expected or experienced.

He had no way to explain it to her, when he was far from understanding it himself.

After pressing a kiss to her shoulder, he lifted his head to look at her. Her eyes were closed, and her face was flushed and utterly relaxed. He wondered if she had any idea how much had changed, for both of them, that morning.

"Are you all right?"

She shook her head, alarming him. Instantly concerned, he braced on his arms to remove his weight from her. Her lashes fluttered up so that he could see the smoky eyes beneath them.

"I'm not all right." Her voice was low and throaty. "I'm wonderful. You're wonderful." The smile curved beautifully on her lips. "This is wonderful."

"You had me worried." He brushed the hair away from her cheek. "I don't think I've ever been quite so nervous." Her lips were waiting for his when he bent his head to kiss her. "You're not sorry?"

Her brow arched. "Do I look sorry?"

"No." Taking his time, he studied her face, tracing it with a fingertip. "You look kind of smug." And the fact that she did brought him a rush of deep satisfaction.

"I'm feeling very smug. And lazy." She stretched a little, so he shifted to let her head rest on his shoulder.

"Happy birthday."

She chuckled against his throat. "It was the most . . . unique present I've ever been given."

"The thing about it is, you can use it over and over again."

"Even better." She tipped her head back, and now her eyes were solemn. "You were very good to me, Boone. Very good for me."

"It wasn't what I'd call an act of altruism. I've wanted this since the first time I saw you."

"I know. It frightened me—and excited me, too." She smoothed her palm over his chest, wishing for a moment they could stay like this forever, cocooned together in the sunlight.

"This changes things."

Her hand stilled, tensed. "Only if you want it to."

"Then I want it to." He sat up, bringing her with him so that they were face-to-face. "I want you to be a part of my life. I want to be with you, as often as possible—and not just like this."

She felt the old, niggling fear trying to surface. Rejection. Rejection now would be devastating. "I am part of your life. I always will be now."

He saw something in her eyes, sensed it in the tension suddenly blooming in the room with them. "But?"

"No buts," she said quickly, and threw her arms around him. "No ands. No anything now. Just this." She kissed him, pouring everything she could into it, knowing she was cheating them both by holding back. Not knowing how to offer it and keep him with her.

"I'm here when you want me, as long as you want me. I promise you."

Rushing her again, he berated himself as she clung to him. How could he expect her to be in love just because they had made love? He wasn't even sure what he was feeling himself. It had all happened too fast, and he was riding on the emotion of the moment. He reminded himself, as he held Ana, that he didn't have only his own needs to consider.

There was Jessie.

What happened with Ana would affect his daughter. So there could be no mistaking, no acting on impulse, and no real commitment until he was sure.

"We'll take it slow," he said, but felt a twinge of resentment when Ana immediately relaxed against him. "But if anyone else comes to your door bearing gifts or needing a cup of sugar—"

"I'll boot him out." She squeezed him hard. "There's no one but you." Turning her head, she pressed her lips to his throat. "You make me happy."

"I can make you happier."

She laughed, tilting her head back. "Really?"

"Not like that." Amused, and flattered, he nipped her lower lip. "Not quite yet, anyway. I was thinking more along the lines of going down and fixing you lunch while you lazed around in bed and waited for me. And then making love with you again. And again."

"Well…" It was tempting, but she recalled too well what one of his meals did to a kitchen. And she had too many jars and bottles around that he might use incorrectly. "Why don't we do it this way—you wait for me while I fix lunch?"

"It's your birthday."

"Exactly." She kissed him before she slid out of bed. "Which is why I get to do everything my own way. I won't be long."

It was a pretty stupid man who wouldn't take a deal like that, Boone decided as he leaned back with his arms crossed under his head. He listened to her running water in the adjoining bath, then settled down to imagine what it would be like to spend the afternoon in bed.

Ana belted her robe as she walked downstairs. Love, she thought, did marvelous things for the spirit. Better, far better, than any potion she could brew or conjure. Perhaps in time, perhaps with enough of that love, she could give him the rest.

Boone wasn't Robert, and she was ashamed to have compared them, even for a moment. But the risk was so great, and the day so marvelous.

Humming to herself, she busied herself in the kitchen. Sandwiches would be best, she decided. Not terribly elegant, but practical for eating in bed. Sandwiches, and some of her father's special wine. She all but floated to the refrigerator, which was crowded now with Jessie's artwork.

"Not even dressed yet," Morgana said through the back screen. "I suspected as much."

With a boneless turkey breast in her hand, Ana turned. Not only was Morgana at her kitchen door, but crowded around her was Nash, Sebastian and Mel, too.

"Oh." She felt the flush blooming even as she set the lunch meat aside. "I didn't hear you drive up."

"Obviously too self-involved, with your birthday and all," Sebastian commented.

They piled in, bringing hugs and kisses and pushing ribboned boxes into her hands. Nash was already opening a bottle of champagne. "Find some glasses, Mel. Let's get this party started." He winked at his wife as she collapsed in a chair. "Apple juice for you, babe."

"I'm too fat to argue." She adjusted her weight—or tried to. "So, did you hear from Ireland?"

"Yes, a chest this morning. It's gorgeous. Glasses in the next cupboard," she told Mel. "Gifts inside. I talked to them…" Right before she'd gone upstairs to make love with Boone. Another flush heated her cheeks. "I, ah, I really need to…" Mel shoved a glass into her hand with champagne brimming up to the lip.

"Have the first glass," Sebastian finished for her. He cocked his head to the side. "Anastasia, my love, you look quite radiant. Turning twenty-seven certainly appears to agree with you."

"Keep out of my head," she muttered, and took a sip to give herself a moment to figure out how to explain. "I can't thank you all enough for coming by this way. If you'd just excuse me a minute."

"No need to get dressed for us." Nash poured the rest of the glasses. "Sebastian's right. You look fabulous."

"Yes, but I really need to—"

"Ana, I have a better idea." The sound of Boone's voice from just down the hall had everyone lapsing into silence. "Why don't we—" Shirtless, barefoot and rumpled, he walked into the room, then stopped dead.

"Whoops," Mel said, and grinned into her glass.

"Succinctly put." Her husband studied Boone through narrowed eyes. "Dropping by for a neighborly visit, are we?"

"Shut up, Sebastian." This from Morgana, who rested both hands on her tummy and smiled. "We seem to have interrupted."

"I think we would have if we'd been any earlier," Nash murmured into Mel's ear, and made her choke back a chuckle.

Ana aimed one withering glance at him before she turned to Boone. "My family's brought along a little party, and they're all quite amused at the idea that I might have a private life—" she looked over her shoulder meaningfully "—that doesn't concern them."

"She always was cranky when you got her out of bed," Sebastian said, resigned to accepting Boone. For now. "Mel, it appears we'll need another glass of champagne."

"Already got it covered." Smiling, she stepped forward and offered it to Boone. "If you can't beat 'em," she said under her breath, and he nodded.

"Well." He took a long sip and sighed. It was obvious that his plans for the rest of the day would have to be adjusted. "Anybody bring cake?"

With a delighted laugh, Morgana gestured toward a large bakery box. "Get Ana a knife, Nash, so she can cut the first piece. I think we'll dispense with candles. She appears to have gotten her wish already."

Chapter Eight

Ana was much too accustomed to her family to be annoyed with or embarrassed by them for long. And she was simply too happy with Boone to hold a grudge. As the days passed, they moved slowly, cautiously, toward cementing their relationship.

If she had come to trust him with her heart, with her body, she had not yet come to trust him with her secrets.

Though his feelings for her had ripened, deepened into a love he had never expected to experience again, he was as wary as she of taking that final step that would join their lives.

At the center was a child neither would have harmed by putting their own needs first.

If they stole a few hours on bright afternoons or rainy mornings, it was theirs to steal. At night Ana would lie alone and wonder how long this magic interlude would last.

As Halloween approached, she and Boone were caught up in their own preparations. Now and again her nerves would jump out at the idea of her lover meeting the whole of her family on the holiday. Then she would laugh at herself for acting like a girl on the point of introducing a first date.

By noon on the thirty-first, she was already at Morgana's, helping her now greatly pregnant cousin with preparations for the Halloween feast.

"I could have made Nash do this." Morgana pressed a hand against the ache in the small of her back before she sat down to knead bread dough from a more comfortable position at the kitchen table.

"You could make Nash do anything simply by asking." Ana cubed lamb for the traditional Irish stew. "But he's having such fun setting up his special effects."

"Just like a layman to think he can outdo the professionals." She winced and moaned and had Ana's immediate attention.

"Honey?"

"No, no, it's not labor, though I damn well wish it was. I'm just so bloody uncomfortable all the time now." Hearing the petulance in her own voice, she winced again. "And I hate whiners."

"You whine all you like. It's just you and me. Here." Always prepared, Ana poured some liquid into a cup. "Drink it down."

"I already feel like I'm going to float away—like Cleopatra's barge. By the goddess, I'm big enough." But she drank, fingering the crystal around her neck.

"And you already have a crew of two."

That did the trick of making her laugh. "Talk to me about something else," she begged, and went back to her kneading. "Anything to take my mind off the fact that I'm fat and grumpy."

"You're not fat, and you're only a little grumpy." But Ana cast her mind around for a distraction. "Did you know that Sebastian and Mel are working on another case together?"

"No, I didn't." And it served to pique her interest. "I'm surprised. Mel's very territorial about her private investigation business."

"Well, she's lowered the gate on this one. A runaway, only twelve years old. The parents are frantic. When I talked to her last night, she said they had a lead, and she was sorry she couldn't take this afternoon off to give you a hand."

"When Mel's in the kitchen, it's more like giving me a foot." There was affection for her new in-law in every syllable. "She's wonderful with Sebastian, isn't she?"

"Yes." Smiling to herself, Ana layered the lamb with potatoes and onions in Morgana's big Dutch oven. "Tough-minded, hardheaded, softhearted. She's exactly what he needs."

"And have you found what you need?"

Saying nothing at first, Ana added herbs. She'd known Morgana would work her way around to it before the day was over. "I'm very happy."

"I like him. I had a good feeling about him from the first."

"I'm glad."

"So does Sebastian—though he has some reservations." Her brows knit, but she kept her voice light.

"Particularly after he cornered Boone and picked through his brain."

Ana's lips thinned as she adjusted the heat on the stove. "I haven't forgiven him for that yet."

"Well." Morgana shrugged and set the dough in a bowl to rise. "Boone didn't know, and it soothed Sebastian's feathers. He wasn't exactly pleased to have walked in on your birthday and found you fresh out of bed."

"It's certainly none of his business."

"He loves you." She gave Ana's arm a quick squeeze as she passed the stove. "He'll always worry about you more because you're the youngest—and simply because your gift makes you so vulnerable."

"I'm not without my defenses, Morgana, or common sense."

"I know. Darling, I..." She felt her eyes fill and brushed hastily at the tears. "It was your first time. I didn't want to probe before, but... Lord, I never used to be so sentimental."

"You were just able to hide it better." Abandoning her cooking for the moment, Ana crossed over to take Morgana into her arms. "It was beautiful, and he's so gentle. I knew there was a reason I had to wait, and he was it." She drew back, smiling. "Boone's given me more than I ever imagined I could have."

With a sigh, Morgana lifted her hands to Ana's face. "You're in love with him."

"Yes. Very much in love with him."

"And he with you?"

Her gaze faltered. "I don't know."

"Oh, Ana."

"I won't link with him that way." Her eyes leveled again, her voice firmed. "It would be dishonest when

I haven't told him what I am, and haven't the courage to tell him how I feel myself. I know he cares for me. I need no gift to know he cares for me. And that's enough. When there's more, if there's more, he'll tell me."

"It never fails to surprise me how damn stubborn you are."

"I'm a Donovan," Ana countered. "And this is important."

"I agree. You should tell him." She gripped Ana's arms before her cousin could turn away. "Oh, I know. I despise it when someone gives me advice I don't want to hear. But you have to let go of the past and face the future."

"I am facing the future. I'd like Boone to be in it. I need more time." Her voice broke, and she pressed her lips together until she felt she could steady it. "Morgana, I know him. He's a good man. He has compassion and imagination and a capacity for generosity he isn't even aware of. He also has a child."

When Ana turned away this time, Morgana was forced to brace herself on the table. "Is that what you're afraid of? Taking on someone else's child?"

"Oh, no. I love her. Who wouldn't? Even before I loved Boone, I loved Jessie. And she's the center of his world, as it should be. There's nothing, absolutely nothing, I wouldn't do for either of them."

"Then explain."

Stalling, Ana rinsed the hard-cooked eggs she was going to devil. "Do you have any fresh dill? You know how Uncle Douglas loves his deviled eggs with dill."

On a hiss of breath, Morgana slapped a jar on the counter. "Anastasia, explain."

Emotions humming, Ana jerked off the tap. "Oh, you don't know how fortunate you are with Nash. To have someone love you that way no matter what."

"Of course I know," Morgana said softly. "What does Nash have to do with this?"

"How many other men would accept one of us so completely? How many would want marriage, or take a witch as a mother for his child?"

"In the name of Finn, Anastasia." The impatience in her voice was spoiled a bit by the fact that she was forced to sit again. "You talk as if we're broomstick-riding crones, cackling while we curdle the milk in a mother's breast."

She didn't smile. "Don't most think of us just that way? Robert—"

"A pox on Robert."

"All right, forget him," Ana agreed with a wave of her hand. "How many times through the centuries have we been hunted and persecuted, feared and ostracized, simply for being what we were born to be? I'm not ashamed of my blood. I don't regret my gift or my heritage. But I couldn't bear it if I told him, and he looked at me as if—" she gave a half laugh "—as if I had a smoking cauldron in the basement filled with toads and wolfsbane."

"If he loves you—"

"If," Ana repeated. "We'll see. Now I think you should lie down for an hour."

"You're just changing the subject," Morgana began, then looked up as Nash burst in. There were cobwebs in his hair—simulated, fortunately—and an unholy gleam in his eyes.

"You guys have got to see this. It's incredible. I'm so good, I scare myself." He snatched a celery stalk from the counter and chomped. "Come on, don't just stand there."

"Amateurs," Morgana sighed, and hauled herself to her feet.

The two women were admiring Nash's hologram ghosts in the foyer when Ana heard a car drive up.

"They're here." Filled with delight at the prospect of seeing her family, she took one bounding leap toward the door. Then stopped dead. She was already whirling around when Morgana sagged against Nash.

Instantly he went as pale as his ghosts. "Babe? Are you—? Oh, boy."

"It's all right." She let out a long breath as Ana took her other arm. "Just a twinge, really." Leaning back against Nash, she smiled at Ana. "I guess having twins on Halloween is pretty appropriate."

"Absolutely nothing to worry about." Douglas Donovan was reassuring Nash. Like his son, he was a tall man, and his mane of raven hair was only lightly silvered. He'd chosen black tie and tails for the occasion, and had set them off with orange neon sneakers that pleased him enormously by glowing in the dark. "Childbirth. Most natural thing in the world. Perfect night for it, too."

"Right." Nash swallowed the lump in his throat. His house was full of people—witches, if you wanted to get technical—and his wife was sitting on the sofa, looking as if she weren't the least bit concerned that she'd been in labor for over three hours. "Maybe it was a false alarm."

Camilla wafted by in a sequined ball gown and tapped Nash on the shoulder with her feather fan. "Leave it to Ana, dear child. She'll take care of everything. Why, when I had Sebastian, I was in labor for thirteen hours. We joked about that, didn't we, Douglas?''

"After you'd stopped shouting curses at me, dear heart."

"Well, naturally." She wandered toward the kitchen, thinking she'd check on the stew. Ana never used quite enough sage.

"Would have turned me into a hedgehog if she hadn't been otherwise occupied," Douglas confided.

"That makes me feel better," Nash muttered. "Heaps."

Delighted to have helped, Douglas slapped him heartily on the back. "That's what we're here for, Dash."

"Nash."

Douglas smiled benignly. "Yes, indeed."

"Mama." Morgana gave her mother's hand a squeeze. "Go rescue poor Nash from Uncle Douglas. He's looking a little queasy."

Bryna obligingly set aside her sketchpad. "Shall I have your father take him out for a walk?"

"Wonderful." She gave a sigh of gratitude as Ana continued to rub her shoulders. "There isn't anything for him to do quite yet."

Ana's father, Padrick, plopped down the moment Bryna vacated the seat. "How's the girl?"

"I'm really fine. It's all very mild as yet, but I'm sure it'll get rolling before too much longer." She leaned over to kiss his plump cheek. "I'm glad you're all here."

"Wouldn't be anywhere else." He put a pudgy hand on her belly to soothe and gave his daughter one of his elvish grins. "And my own little darling. You're pretty as a picture. Take right after your da, don't you?"

"Naturally." Ana felt the next contraction start and kept her hands steady on Morgana's shoulders. "Long, relaxed breaths, love."

"Will you want to give her some blue cohosh?" he asked his daughter.

Ana considered, then shook her head. "Not yet. She's doing well enough. But you could get me my pouch. I'll want some crystals."

"Done." He rose, then flipped his hand over. In the palm was a sprig of bell heather in full flower. "Now where did this come from?" he said, in the way he had since the laboring woman had been a babe herself. "Take care of this for me. I've business to tend to."

Morgana brushed the heather against her cheek. "He's the dearest man in the world."

"He'll spoil these two if you let him. Da's a pushover for children." With the empathic link, she knew Morgana was in more discomfort than she was letting on. "I'll have to take you upstairs soon, Morgana."

"Not yet, though." She reached over her shoulder for Ana's hand. "It's so nice being here with everyone. Where's Aunt Maureen?"

"Mama's in the kitchen, probably arguing with Aunt Camilla over the stew by now."

On a little groan, Morgana shut her eyes. "Lord, I could eat a gallon of it."

"After," Ana promised, and looked up as the rattle of chains and the moans of the suffering filled the room. "Somebody at the door."

"Poor Nash. He can't relax long enough to appreciate his own handiwork. Is it Sebastian?"

Ana craned her neck. "Uh-huh. He and Mel are critiquing the holograms. Whoops, there goes the smoke machine and the bats."

Sebastian strode in. "Amateurs."

"And Lydia was so scared she screamed and screamed," Jessie said, relating the chills and thrills of the elementary school's haunted house. "Then Frankie ate so much candy he threw up."

"Sounds like a red-letter day." To forestall exactly the same eventuality, he'd already hidden away half of the treats Jessie'd collected in her goodie bag.

"I like my costume best of all." As they got out of the car in front of Morgana's, Jessie twirled so that the starry pink material floated around her. Rather pleased with himself, Boone crouched to adjust her wings of aluminum foil. It had taken him the better part of two days to figure out how to tack and baste and tie the fairy costume together. But it was worth it.

She tapped her father's shoulder with her cardboard wand. "Now you're the handsome prince."

"What was I before?"

"The ugly toad." She squealed with laughter as he tweaked her nose. "Do you think Ana's going to be surprised? Will she recognize me?"

"Not a chance. I'm not sure I recognize you myself." They'd opted to dispense with a mask, and Boone had painted her cheeks with rouge, reddened her lips, and smudged her eyelids up to her eyebrows with glittery gold shadow.

"We're going to meet her whole family," she reminded her father—as if he needed reminding. He'd been worrying about the event all week. "And I get to see Morgana's cat and dog again."

"Right." He tried not to be overly concerned about the dog. Pan might look like a wolf—disconcertingly so—but he'd been gentle and friendly with Jessie the last time they'd visited.

"This is going to be the best Halloween party in the whole world." Rising to her tiptoes, she pushed the doorbell. Her mouth fell open in a soundless gasp when the moans and clanking chains filled the air.

A husky man with thinning hair and jolly eyes opened the door. He took one look at Jessie and spoke in his best ghoul's voice. "Welcome to the haunted castle. Enter at your own risk."

Her eyes were big blue saucers. "Is it really haunted?"

"Come in... if you dare." He squatted down until he was at eye level with her, then pulled a fluffy stuffed bunny from up his sleeve.

"Ooh..." Charmed, Jessie pressed it against her cheek. "Are you a magician?"

"Certainly. Isn't everyone?"

"Uh-uh. I'm a fairy princess."

"That's good enough. And is this your escort for the evening?" he asked, glancing up at Boone.

"No." Jessie laughed gaily. "He's my daddy. I'm really Jessie."

"I'm really Padrick."

He straightened, and though his eyes remained merry, Boone was sure he was being measured. "And you'd be?"

"Sawyer." He offered a hand. "Boone Sawyer. We're Anastasia's neighbors."

"Neighbors, you say? Well, I doubt that's all. But come in, come in." He exchanged Boone's hand for Jessie's. "See what we have in store for you."

"Ghosts!" She nearly bounced out of her Mary Janes. "Daddy, ghosts!"

"Not a bad attempt for a layman," Padrick said kindly enough. "Oh, by the way, Ana's just taken Nash and Morgana upstairs. We're having twins tonight. Maureen, my passion flower, come meet Ana's neighbors." He turned to Boone as a striking amazon in a scarlet turban came striding down the hall.

"I imagine you'd like a drink, boyo," Padrick said to Boone.

"Yes, sir." Boone blew out a long breath. "I believe I would."

Hesitant and uneasy, Mel knocked on the door of Morgana's bedroom, then poked her head in. She wasn't sure whether she'd expected the clinical—and, to her mind, frightening—aura of a delivery room or the mystical glow of a magic circle. Either one she could have done without.

Instead, there was Morgana propped up in a big, cozy-looking bed, flowers and candles all around. Harp and flute music was drifting through the room. Morgana looked a bit flushed, Nash more than a bit pale, but the basic normality of it all reassured Mel enough to have her crossing the threshold when Ana gestured to her.

"Come on in, Mel. You should be an expert at this now. After all, you helped Sebastian and me deliver the foal just a few months ago."

"I feel like a horse," Morgana muttered, "but that doesn't mean I appreciate the comparison."

"I don't want to interrupt, or get in the way or— Oh, boy," she whispered when Morgana threw her head back and began to puff like a steam engine.

"Okay, okay." Nash gripped her hand and fumbled with a stopwatch. "Here comes another one. We're doing fine, just fine."

"We, hell," Morgana said between her teeth. "I'd like to see you—"

"Breathe." Ana's voice was gentle as she placed crystals over Morgana's belly. They hovered in the air, gleaming with an unearthly light that Mel tried to take in stride.

After all, she reminded herself, she'd been married to a witch for two months.

"It's all right, babe." Nash pressed his lips to her hand, wishing desperately for the pain to pass. "It's almost over."

"Don't go." She gripped his hand hard as the contraction began to ease. "Don't go."

"I'm right here. You're wonderful." As Ana had instructed him, he cooled Morgana's face with a damp cloth. "I love you, gorgeous."

"You'd better." She managed a smile and let out a long, cleansing breath. Knowing she had a ways to go, she closed her eyes. "How am I doing, Ana?"

"Great. A couple more hours."

"A couple—" Nash bit off the words and fixed on a smile that was sick around the edges. "Terrific."

Mel cleared her throat, and Ana glanced over. "I'm sorry. We got a little distracted."

"No problem. I just thought you'd want to know Boone's here—with Jessie."

"Oh." Ana mopped her own brow with her shirtsleeve. "I'd forgotten. I'll be right down. Would you send Aunt Bryna up?"

"Sure. Hey, Morgana, we're all with you."

Morgana's smile was just a tad wicked. "Great. Want to change places?"

"I'll pass this time, thanks." She was edging toward the door. "I'll just get out of your way."

"You're not going to be gone long." Struggling against panic, Nash rubbed the small of Morgana's back and looked pleadingly at Ana.

"Only a minute or two. And Aunt Bryna's very skilled. Besides, we need some brandy."

"Brandy? She's not supposed to drink."

"For you," Ana said gently as she slipped out of the room.

The first thing Ana noted when she reached the parlor was that Jessie was being very well entertained. Ana's mother was laughing her lusty, full-bodied laugh as Jessie recounted her class's escapades at the school Halloween party. Since Jessie was already cuddling two stuffed animals, Ana deduced that her father had already been up to his tricks.

She certainly hoped he'd been discreet.

"Things are well upstairs?" Bryna said quietly as they passed in the doorway.

"Perfect. You'll be a grandmother before midnight."

"Bless you, Anastasia." Bryna kissed her cheek. "And I do like your young man."

"He's not—" But her aunt was already hurrying upstairs.

And there was Boone standing by the fireplace, where the flames crackled cheerily, drinking what was surely one of her father's concoctions and listening, with an expression of fascinated bemusement, to one of her Uncle Douglas's stories.

"So, naturally, we took the poor soul in for the night. Storm being what it was. And what did he do but go screeching out in the morning, shouting about banshees and ghosts and the like. Touched," Douglas said sadly, tapping a finger to his head, where an orange silk hat now resided. "A sad and sorry tale."

"Perhaps it had something to do with you clanging about in that suit of armor," Matthew Donovan commented, warming a brandy in his long-fingered hands.

"No, no, a suit of armor doesn't resemble a banshee in the least. I imagine it was Maureen's cat screeching that did it."

"My cats do not screech," she said, insulted. "They're quite well behaved."

"I have a dog," Jessie piped up. "But I like cats, too."

"Is that so?" Always willing to oblige, Padrick plucked a yellow-striped stuffed kitten from between her fairy wings. "How about this one?"

"Oh!" Jessie buried her face in its fur, then delighted Padrick by climbing onto his lap and kissing his rosy cheek.

"Da." Ana leaned over the sofa to press her lips to his balding head. "You never change."

"Ana!" Jessie bounced on Padrick's lap and tried to hold up her entire menagerie at once. "Your daddy's the funniest person in the world!"

"I like him myself." She tilted her head curiously. "But who are you?"

"I'm Jessie." Giggling, she climbed down to turn in a circle.

"No, really?"

"Honest. Daddy made me a fairy princess for Halloween."

"You certainly sound like Jessie." Ana crouched down. "Give me a kiss and let's see."

Jessie pressed her painted lips to Ana's, flushing with pleasure at her costume's success. "Didn't you know me? Really?"

"You fooled me completely. I was certain you were a real fairy princess."

"Your daddy said you were his fairy princess 'cause your mama was a queen."

Maureen let out another peal of laughter, and winked at her husband. "My little frog."

"I'm sorry I can't stay and talk," Ana told Jessie.

"I know. You're helping get Morgana's babies out. Do they come out together or one at a time?"

"One at a time, I hope." She laughed, tousling Jessie's hair, and looked over at Boone. "You know you're welcome to stay as long as you like. There's plenty of food."

"Don't worry about us. How's Morgana?"

"Very well. Actually, I came down to get some brandy for Nash. His nerves are about shot."

With an understanding nod, Matthew picked up a decanter and a snifter. "He has my sympathy." When he passed them to her, she felt a jolt of his power and knew that, however calm his exterior, his mind and his heart were upstairs with his daughter.

"Don't worry. I'll take care of her, Uncle Matthew."

"No one better. You are the best I've known, Anastasia." His eyes held hers as he flicked a finger over the bloodstone she wore around her neck. "And I've known many." Then a smile touched his lips. "Boone, perhaps you'd walk Anastasia back up."

"Be glad to." Boone took the decanter from Ana before they started out.

"Your family," Boone began, shaking his head at the foot of the stairs, unaware that she'd stiffened.

"Yes?"

"Incredible. Absolutely incredible. It isn't every day I find myself plopped into the center of a group of strangers, with a woman about to give birth to twins upstairs, a wolf—because I swear that dog is no dog— gnawing what looks like a mastodon bone under the kitchen table, and mechanical bats flying overhead. Oh, I forgot the ghosts in the foyer."

"Well, it is Halloween."

"I don't think that has much to do with it." He stopped at the top of the stairs. "I can't remember ever being more entertained. They're fabulous, Ana. Your father does these magic tricks—terrific magic tricks. For the life of me I couldn't figure out how he pulled it off."

"No, you wouldn't. He's, ah...very accomplished."

"He could make a living at it. I've got to tell you, I wouldn't have missed this party for the world." He cupped his free hand around her neck. "The only thing missing is you."

"I was worried you'd feel awkward."

"No. Though it does kind of scotch my plans to lure you into some shadowy corner and make you shiver with some bloodcurdling story so you'd climb all over me for protection."

"I don't spook easily." Smiling, she twined her arms around him. "I grew up on bloodcurdling."

"And uncles clanging around in suits of armor," he murmured as he brushed his lips over hers.

"Oh, that's the least of it." She leaned against him, changing the angle of the kiss. "We used to play in the dungeons. And I spent an entire night in the haunted tower on one of Sebastian's dares."

"Courageous."

"No, stubborn. And stupid. I've never been more uncomfortable in my life." She was drifting into the kiss, losing herself. "At least until Morgana conjured up a blanket and pillow."

"Conjured?" he repeated, amused by the term.

"Sent up," she corrected, and poured herself into the embrace so that he would think of nothing but her.

When the door opened beside them, they looked around like guilty children. Bryna lifted her brows, summed up the situation and smiled.

"I'm sorry to interrupt, but I think Boone is just what we need right now."

He took a firmer grip on the brandy bottle. "In there?"

She laughed. "No. If you'd just stay there, and let me send Nash out for a moment or two. He could use a little man talk."

"Only for a minute," Ana cautioned. "Morgana needs him inside."

Before Boone could agree or refuse, she slipped away. Resigned, he poured a snifter, took a good swallow himself, then refilled it when Nash stepped out.

He pressed the snifter on Nash. "Have a shot."

"I didn't think it would take so long." After a long breath, he sipped the brandy. "Or that it would hurt her so much. If we get through this, I swear, I'm never going to touch her again.''

''Yeah, right.''

''I mean it.'' Despite the fact he knew it was an expectant-father cliché, he began to pace.

''Nash, I don't mean to interfere, but wouldn't you feel better—safer—if Morgana was in a hospital, with a doctor and all that handy medical business?''

''A hospital? No.'' Nash rubbed a hand over his face. ''Morgana was born in that same bed. She wouldn't have it any other way with the twins. I guess I wouldn't, either.''

''Well, a doctor, then.''

''Ana's the best.'' Remembering that relaxed him slightly. ''Believe me, Morgana couldn't be in better hands than hers.''

''I know midwives are supposed to be excellent, and more natural, I imagine.'' He moved his shoulders. If Nash was content with the situation, it wasn't up to him to worry about it. ''I guess she's done it before.''

''No, this is Morgana's first time.''

''I meant Ana,'' Boone said on a chuckle. ''Delivering babies.''

''Oh, yeah. Sure. She knows what she's doing. It's not that. In fact, I think I'd go crazy if she wasn't here. But—'' He took another swallow, paced a little more. ''I mean, this has been going on for hours. I don't know how she can stand it. I don't know why any woman stands it. Just seems to me she could do something about it. Damn it, she's a witch.''

Manfully masking another chuckle, he gave Nash an encouraging pat on the back. ''Nash, it's not a good time to call her names. Women get a little nasty when they're in labor. They're entitled.''

"No, I mean—" He broke off, realizing he was going over the edge. "I've got to pull myself together."

"Yep."

"I know it's going to be all right. Ana wouldn't let anything happen. But it's so hard to watch her hurting."

"When you love someone, it's the hardest thing in the world. But you get through it. And, in this case, you're getting something fantastic out of it."

"I never thought I could feel this way, about anybody. She's everything."

"I know what you mean."

Feeling better, Nash passed the snifter back to Boone. "Is that how it is with Ana?"

"I think it might be. I know she's special."

"Yeah, she is." Nash hesitated, and when he spoke again he chose his words with care. Loyalty, split two ways, was the heaviest of burdens. "You'd be able to understand her, Boone, with your imagination, your way of looking beyond what's considered reality. She is a very special lady, with qualities that make her different from anyone you've ever known. If you love her, and you want her to be a part of your life and Jessie's, don't let those qualities block you."

Boone's brows drew together. "I don't think I'm following you."

"Just remember I said it. Thanks for the drink." He took a steadying breath, then went back in to his wife.

Chapter Nine

"**B**reathe. Come on, baby, breathe!"

"I am breathing." Morgana grunted out the words between pants and couldn't quite manage to glare at Nash. "What the hell do you call this if it's not breathing?"

Nash figured he was past his own crisis point. She'd already called him every name in the book, and had invented several more. Ana said they were nearly there, and he was clinging to that as desperately as Morgana was clinging to his hand. So he merely smiled at his sweaty wife and mopped her brow with a cool cloth.

"Growling, spitting, snarling." He touched his lips to hers, relieved when she didn't bite him. "You're not going to turn me into a slug or a two-headed newt, are you?"

She laughed, groaned, and let out the last puff of air. "I can come up with something much more inventive. I need to sit up more. Ana?"

"Nash, get in the bed behind her. Support her back. It's going to go quickly now." Arching her own back, which echoed the aches in Morgana's, she checked one last time to see if all was ready. There were blankets warmed by the fire, heated water, the clamps and scissors already sterilized, the glow of crystals pulsing with power.

Bryna stood by her daughter's side, her eyes bright with understanding and concern. Images of her own hours in that same bed fighting to bring life into the world raced through her head. That same bed, she thought blinking at the mists in her eyes, where her child now labored through the last moments, the last pangs.

"No pushing until I tell you. Pant. Pant," Ana repeated as she felt the contraction build within herself—a sweet and terrible pang that brought fresh sweat to her skin. Morgana stiffened, fought off the need to tense, and struggled to do as she was told. "Good, good. Nearly there, darling, I promise. Have you picked out names?"

"I like Curly and Moe," Nash said, panting right along with Morgana until she managed to jab him weakly with an elbow. "Okay, okay, Ozzie and Harriet, but only if we have one of each."

"Don't make me laugh now, you idiot." But she did laugh, and the pain eased back. "I want to push. I have to push."

"If it's two girls," he continued, with an edge of desperation, "we're going with Lucy and Ethel." He pressed his cheek against hers.

"Two boys and it's Boris and Bela." Morgana's laughter took on a slightly hysterical note as she reached back to link her arms around Nash's neck. "God, Ana, I have to—"

"Bear down," Ana snapped out. "Go ahead, push."

Caught between laughter and tears, Morgana threw her head back and fought to bring life into the room. "Oh, God!" Outside, lightning shot across a cloudless sky and thunder cracked its celestial whip.

"Nice going, champ," Nash began, but then his mind seemed to go blank as glass. "Look! Oh, Lord, would you look at that!"

At the foot of the bed, Ana gently, competently turned the tiny, dark head. "Hold back now, honey. I know it's hard, but hold back just for a minute. Pant. That's it, that's the way. Next time's the charm."

"It's got hair," Nash said weakly. His face was as wet with sweat and tears as Morgana's. "Just look at that. What is it?"

"I haven't got that end out yet." Ana sent a glittering smile to her cousin. "Okay, this is for the grand prize. Bear down, honey, and let's see if we've got Ozzie or Harriet."

With laughter, Morgana delivered her child into Ana's waiting hands. As the first wild, indignant cry of life echoed in the room, Nash buried his face in his wife's tangled hair.

"Morgana. Sweet Lord, Morgana. Ours."

"Ours." The pain was already forgotten. Eyes glowing, Morgana held out her arms so that Ana could place the tiny, wriggling bundle into them. In the language of her blood, she murmured to the babe, as her hands moved gently to welcome.

"What is it?" With a trembling hand, Nash reached down to touch the tiny head. "I forgot to look."

"You have a son," Ana told him.

At the first lusty wail, conversation in the parlor downstairs cut off like a switch. All eyes shifted to the stairs. There was silence, stillness. Touched, Boone looked at his own child, who slept peacefully on the sofa, her head nestled in Padrick's comfortable lap.

He felt a tremor beneath his feet, saw the wine slosh back and forth in his glass. Before he could speak, Douglas was removing his top hat and slapping Matthew on the back.

"A new Donovan," he said, and snatched up a glass to lift in toast. "A new legacy."

A little teary-eyed, Camilla walked over to kiss her brother-in-law's cheek. "Blessed be."

Boone was about to add his congratulations when Sebastian crossed the room. He lighted a white candle, then a gold one. Taking up a bottle of unopened wine, he broke the seal, then poured pale gold liquid into an ornate silver chalice.

"A star dawns in the night. Life from life, blood through blood to shine its light. Through love he was given the gift of birth, and from breath to death will walk the earth. The other gift comes through blood and bone, and is for him to take and own. Charm of the moon, power of the sun. Never forgetting an it harm none."

Sebastian passed the cup to Matthew, who sipped first. Fascinated, Boone watched the Donovans pass the chalice of wine from one to the other. An Irish tradition? he wondered. It was certainly more moving, more charming, than passing out cigars.

When he was handed the cup, he was both honored and baffled. Even as he began to sip, another wail sounded, announcing another life.

"Two stars," Matthew said in a voice thickened with pride. "Two gifts."

Then the solemn mood was broken as Padrick conjured up a party streamer and a rain of confetti. As he blew a celebratory toot, his wife laughed bawdily.

"Happy New Year," she said gesturing toward the clock that had just begun to strike twelve. "It's the best All Hallows' Eve since Padrick made the pigs fly." She grinned at Boone. "He's such a prankster."

"Pigs," Boone began, but the group turned as one as Bryna entered the room. She moved directly to her husband, who folded her tightly within his arms.

"They're all well." She brushed at happy tears. "All well and beautiful. We have a grandson and a granddaughter, my love. And our daughter invites us all upstairs to welcome them."

Not wanting to intrude, Boone hung back as the group piled out of the room. Sebastian stopped in the doorway, arched a brow. "Aren't you coming?"

"I think the family..."

"You were accepted," Sebastian said shortly, not certain he agreed with the rest of the Donovans. He hadn't forgotten how deeply Ana had once been hurt.

"An odd way to phrase it." Boone kept his voice mild to counteract a sudden flare of temper. "Particularly since you feel differently."

"Regardless." Sebastian inclined his head in what Boone interpreted as both challenge and warning. But when Sebastian glanced toward the sofa, he softened. "I imagine Jessie would be disappointed if you didn't wake her and bring her up for a look."

"But you'd rather I didn't."

"Ana would rather you did," Sebastian countered. "And that's more to the point." He moved to the doorway again, then stopped. "You'll hurt her. Anastasia sheds no tears, but she'll shed them for you. Because I love her, I'll have to forgive you for that."

"I don't see—"

"No." Sebastian nodded curtly. "But I do. Bring the child, Sawyer, and join us. It's a night for kindness, and small miracles."

Uncertain why Sebastian's words angered him so much, Boone stared at the empty doorway. He damn well didn't have to prove himself to some overprotective, interfering cousin. When Jessie shifted and blinked owlishly, he pushed Sebastian out of his mind.

"Daddy?"

"Right here, frog face." He bent and lifted his child into his arms. "Guess what?"

She rubbed her eyes. "I'm sleepy."

"We'll go home soon, but I think there's something you'd like to see first." While she yawned and dropped her heavy head on his shoulder, he carried her upstairs.

They were all gathered around, making a great deal more noise than Boone imagined was the norm even for a home delivery room. Nash was sitting on the edge of the bed beside Morgana, holding a tiny bundle and grinning like a fool.

"He looks like me, don't you think?" he was asking of no one in particular. "The nose. He's got my nose."

"That's Allysia," Morgana informed him, rubbing a cheek over her son's downy head. "I've got Donovan."

"Right. Well, *she's* got my nose." He peeked over at his son. "He's got my chin."

"The Donovan chin," Douglas corrected. "Plain as a pikestaff."

"Hah." Maureen was jockeying for position. "They're both Corrigans through and through. Our side of the family has always had strong genes."

While they argued over that, Jessie shook off sleep and stretched forward. "Is it the babies? Did they get born? Can I see?"

"Let the child in." Padrick elbowed his brother out of the way. "Let her have a look."

Jessie kept one arm hooked around her father's neck as she leaned forward. "Oh!" Her tired eyes went bright as Ana took a babe in each arm to hold them up for Jessie to see. "They look just like little faeries." Very delicately, she touched a fingertip to one cheek, then the other.

"That's just what they are." Padrick kissed Jessie's nose. "A brand new faerie prince and princess."

"But they don't have wings," Jessie said, giggling.

"Some faeries don't need wings." Padrick winked at his daughter. "Because they have wings on their hearts."

"These faeries need some rest and some quiet." Ana turned to tuck the babies into Morgana's waiting arms. "And so does their mama."

"I feel wonderful."

"Nevertheless..." Ana shot a warning look over her shoulder that had the Donovans reluctantly filing out.

"Boone," Morgana called out. "Would you wait for Ana, drive her home? She's exhausted."

"I'm perfectly fine. He should—"

"Of course I will." He settled the yawning Jessie on his shoulder. "We'll be downstairs whenever you're ready."

It took another fifteen minutes before Ana was assured that Nash had all her instructions. Morgana was already drifting off to sleep when Ana closed the door and left the new family alone.

She was exhausted, and the powers of the crystals in her pouch were nearly depleted. For almost twelve hours, she had gone through the labor of childbirth with her cousin, as closely linked as it was possible to be. Her body was heavy with fatigue, her mind drugged with it. It was a common result of a strong empathic link.

She staggered once at the top of the stairs, righted herself, then gripped her bloodstone amulet to draw on the last of its strength.

By the time she reached the parlor, she was feeling a little steadier. There was Boone, half dozing in a chair by the fire, with Jessie cuddled against his chest. His eyes opened. His lips curved.

"Hey, champ. I have to admit I thought this whole setup was a little loony, but you did a hell of a job up there."

"It's always stunning to bring life into the world. You didn't have to stay all this time."

"I wanted to." He kissed Jessie's head. "So did she. She'll be the hit of school on Monday with this story."

"It's been a long night for her, and one she won't forget." Ana rubbed her eyes, almost as Jessie had before falling asleep again. "Where is everyone?"

"In the kitchen, raiding the refrigerator and getting drunk. I decided to pass, since I already had more than my share of wine." He offered a sheepish grin.

"A little while ago I could have sworn the house was shaking, so I switched to coffee." He gestured toward the cup on the table beside him.

"And now you'll be up half the night. I'll just run and tell them I'm going, if you'd like to go put Jessie in the car."

Outside, Boone took a deep gulp of the cool night air. Ana was right, he was wide awake. He'd have to work a couple of hours until the coffee wore off, and he'd more than likely pay for it tomorrow. But it had been worth it. He glanced over his shoulder to where the light glowed in Morgana's bedroom. It had been well worth it.

He slipped Jessie's wings over her shoulders, then laid her on the back seat.

"Beautiful night," Ana murmured from behind him. "I think every star must be out."

"Two new stars." Bemused, Boone opened the door for her. "That's what Matthew said. It was really lovely. Sebastian made a toast about life and gifts and stars, and they all passed around a cup of wine. Is that an Irish thing?"

"In a way." She leaned her head back against the seat as he started the car. Within seconds, she was asleep.

When Boone pulled up in his driveway, he wondered how he was going to manage to carry both of them to bed. He shifted, easing his door open, but Ana was already blinking awake.

"Just let me carry her inside, and I'll give you a hand."

"No, I'm fine." Bleary-eyed, Ana stepped out of the car. "I'll help you with her." She laughed as she gathered up the store of stuffed animals. "Da always goes overboard. I hope you don't mind."

"Are you kidding? He was great with her. Come on, baby." He lifted her and, in the way of children, she remained utterly lax. "She was taken with your mother, too, and the rest, but your father was definitely the hero. I expect she'll be bugging me to go to Ireland now, so she can visit him in his castle."

"He'd love it." She took the silver wings and followed him into the house.

"Just set those anywhere. Do you want a brandy?"

"No, really." She dropped the animals on the couch, put the wings beside them, then rolled her aching shoulders. "I wouldn't mind some tea. I can brew some while you settle her in."

"Fine. I won't be long."

A low growling emerged from under Jessie's bed when Boone carried her in. "Great watchdog. It's just us, you blockhead."

Desperately relieved, Daisy bounded out, tail wagging. She waited until Boone had removed Jessie's shoes and costume, then leapt onto the bed to settle at Jessie's feet.

"You wake me up at six and I'll staple those doggie lips closed."

Daisy thumped her tail and shut her eyes.

"I don't know why we couldn't have gotten a smart dog while we were at it," Boone was saying as he walked into the kitchen. "It wouldn't have been . . ." and then his words trailed off.

The kettle was on and beginning to steam. Cups were set out, and the pot was waiting. Ana had her head pillowed on her arms at the kitchen table, and was deep in sleep.

Under the bright light, her lashes cast shadows on her cheeks. Boone hoped it was the harshness of the light that made her look so delicately pale. Her hair spilled over her shoulder. Her lips were soft, just parted.

Looking at her, he thought of the young princess who had been put under a spell by a jealous faerie and made to sleep a hundred years, until wakened by true love's gentle kiss.

"Anastasia. You're so beautiful." He touched her hair, indulging himself. He'd never watched her sleep, and he had a sudden, tearing urge to have her in his bed, to be able to open his eyes in the morning and see her there beside him. "What am I going to do?"

Sighing, he let his hand fall away from her hair and moved to the stove to shut off the kettle. As gently as he had with Jessie, he lifted her into his arms, and, like Jessie, she remained lax. Gritting his teeth against the knots in his stomach, he carried her upstairs and laid her on his bed.

"You don't know how much I've wanted you here," he said under his breath as he slipped off her shoes. "In my bed, in the night. All night." He spread the covers over her, and she sighed, shifting in sleep and curling into his pillow.

The knots in his stomach loosened as he bent to touch his lips to hers. "Good night, princess."

In her panties and T-shirt, Jessie padded into the bedroom before dawn. She'd had a dream, a bad one about the haunted house at school, and wanted the comfort and warmth of her father.

He always made monsters go away.

She scurried to the bed, and climbed in to burrow against him. It was then that she noted it wasn't her father at all, but Ana.

Fascinated, Jessie curled up. Curious fingers played with Ana's hair. In sleep Ana murmured and tucked Jessie under her arm to snuggle her close. Odd sensations tugged through Jessie's stomach. Different smells, different textures, and yet she felt as loved and safe as she did when her father cuddled her. She rested her head trustingly against Ana's breast and slept.

When Ana woke, she felt arms around her, small, limp arms. Disoriented, she stared down at Jessie, then looked around the room.

Not her room, she realized. And not Jessie's. Boone's.

She kept the child warm against her as she tried to piece together what had happened.

The last thing she remembered was sitting down after she'd put on water for tea. Tired, she'd been so tired. She'd rested her head for a moment and . . . and obviously had fallen fast asleep.

So where was Boone?

Cautiously she turned her head, unsure whether she was relieved or disappointed to find the bed beside her empty. Impractical, of course, given the circumstances, but it would have been so lovely to be able to cuddle back against him even as the child cuddled to her.

When she looked back, Jessie's eyes were open and on hers.

"I had a bad dream," the girl told her in hushed morning whispers. "About the Headless Horseman. He was laughing and laughing and chasing me."

Ana snuggled down to kiss Jessie's brow. "I bet he didn't catch you."

"Uh-uh. I woke up and came to get Daddy. He always makes the monsters go away. The ones in the closet and under the bed and at the window and everywhere."

"Daddies are good at that." She smiled, remembering how her own had pretended to chase them away with a magic broom every night during her sixth year.

"But you were here, and I wasn't scared with you, either. Are you going to sleep in Daddy's bed at night now?"

"No." She brushed a hand through Jessie's hair. "I think you and I both fell asleep, and your father had to put both of us to bed."

"But it's a big bed," Jessie pointed out. "There'd be room. I have Daisy to sleep with me now, but Daddy has to sleep all alone. Does Quigley sleep with you?"

"Sometimes," Ana said, relieved at the rapid change of topic. "He's probably wondering where I am."

"I think he knows," Boone announced from the doorway. He was wearing only jeans, unsnapped at the waist, and he looked bleary-eyed and harassed, with the gray cat winding between his legs. "He howled and scratched at the back door until I let him in."

"Oh." Ana shoved her tumbled hair back as she sat up. "Sorry. I guess he woke you."

"Right the first time." He tucked his thumbs in his pockets while the cat leapt onto the bed and began to mutter and complain to his mistress. The knots in his stomach were back, doubled. How could he explain what he felt on seeing Ana cuddled with his little girl in the big, soft bed? "Jessie, what are you doing?"

"I had a bad dream." She leaned her head against Ana's arm and stroked the cat's fur. "So I came in to get you, but Ana was here. She made the monsters go away just like you do." Quigley meowed plaintively and made Jessie giggle. "He's hungry. Poor kitty. I can feed him. Can I take him down and feed him?"

"Sure, if you'd like."

Before Ana had finished the sentence, Jessie was bounding off the bed, calling to the cat to follow.

"Sorry she woke you." Boone hesitated, then moved over to sit on the edge of the bed.

"She didn't. Apparently she just climbed right on in and went back to sleep. And I should apologize for putting you to so much trouble. You could have given me a shake and sent me home."

"You were exhausted." He reached out, much as Jessie had, to touch her hair. "Incredibly beautiful, and totally exhausted."

"Having babies is tiring work." She smiled. "Where did you sleep?"

"In the guest room." He winced at the crick in his back. "Which makes getting a decent bed in there a top priority."

Automatically she pressed her hands on his lower back to massage and ease. "You could have dumped me in there. I don't think I would have known the difference between a bed and a sheet of plywood."

"I wanted you in my bed." His gaze met hers and locked. "I very much wanted you in my bed." He tugged on her hair to bring her closer. Much closer. "I still do."

His mouth was on hers, not so patient now, not so gentle. Ana felt a quick thrill of excitement and alarm as he pressed her back against the pillows. "Boone—"

"Just for a minute." His voice took on an edge of desperation. "I need a minute with you."

He took her breast, searing her flesh through the thin silk of her rumpled blouse. While his hands skimmed over her, his mouth took and took, swallowing her muffled moans. His body ached to cover hers, to press hard against soft, to take quickly, even savagely, what he knew she could bring to him.

"Ana." His teeth scraped down her throat before he gathered her close, just to hold her. He knew he was being unfair, to both of them, and he struggled to back off. "How long does it take to feed that cat?"

"Not long enough." With a shaky laugh, she dropped her head on his shoulder. "Not nearly long enough."

"I was afraid of that." He drew back, running his hands down her arms to take hers. "Jessie's been after me to let her spend the night at Lydia's. If I can work it out, will you stay with me? Here?"

"Yes." She brought his hand to her lips, then pressed it to her cheek. "Whenever you like."

"Tonight." He forced himself to release her, to move away. "Tonight," he repeated. "I'll go call Lydia's mother. Beg if I have to." He steadied himself and slowed down. "I promised Jess we'd go get some ice cream, maybe have lunch on the wharf. Will you come with us? If it all works out, we could drop her off at Lydia's, then go out to dinner."

She pushed off the bed herself, brushing uselessly at the wrinkles in her blouse and slacks. "That sounds nice."

"Great. Sorry about the clothes. I wasn't quite brave enough to undress you."

She felt a quick thrill at the image of him unbuttoning her blouse. Slowly, very slowly, his fingers patient, his eyes hot. She cleared her throat. "They'll press out. I need to change, go check on Morgana and the twins."

"I could drive you."

"That's all right. My father's going to pick me up so I can get my car. What time did you want to leave?"

"About noon, in a couple hours."

"Perfect. I'll meet you back here."

He caught her to him before she reached the doorway, then stopped her heart with another greedy kiss. "Maybe we could pick up some takeout, bring it back and eat here."

"That sounds nice, too," she murmured as she shifted the angle of the kiss. "Or maybe we could just send out for pizza when we get hungry."

"Better. Much better."

By four o'clock, Jessie was standing in Lydia's doorway waving a cheery goodbye. Her pink backpack was bulging with the amazing assortment of necessities a six-year-old girl required for a sleepover. What made the entire matter perfect in her eyes was that Daisy had been invited along for the party.

"Tell me not to feel guilty," Boone asked as he cast one last glance in the rearview mirror.

"About?"

"About wanting my own daughter out of the house tonight."

"Boone." Adoring him, Ana leaned over to kiss his cheek. "You know perfectly well Jessie could hardly wait for us to drive away so she could begin her little adventure at Lydia's."

"Yeah, but... It's not packing her off so much, it's packing her off with ulterior motives."

Knowing what those motives were brought a little knot of heat to Ana's stomach. "She isn't going to have less of a good time because of them—particularly when you promised her she could have a slumber party in a couple of weeks. If you're still feeling guilty think about how you're going to feel riding herd on five or six little girls all night."

He slanted her a look. "I kind of figured you'd help—since you have ulterior motives, too."

"Did you?" The fact that he'd asked pleased her enormously. "Maybe I will." She laid a hand over his. "For a paranoid father riddled with guilt, you're doing a wonderful job."

"Keep it up. I'm feeling better."

"Too much flattery isn't good for you."

"Just for that I won't tell you how many guys gave themselves whiplash craning their necks to get a second look at you when we were walking on the wharf today."

"Oh?" She skimmed back her blowing hair. "Were there many?"

"Depends on how you define many. Besides, too much flattery isn't good for you. I guess I could say I don't know how you could look so good today after the night you put in."

"It could be because I slept like a rock." She stretched luxuriously. A bracelet of agates winked at her wrist. "Morgana's the amazing one. When I got there this morning, she was nursing both of the twins and looking as if she'd just spent a reviving week at an expensive spa."

"The babies okay?"

"The babies are terrific. Healthy and bright-eyed. Nash is already a pro at changing diapers. He claims both of them have smiled at him."

He knew that feeling, too, and had just realized he missed it. "He's a good guy."

"Nash is very special."

"I have to admit, I was stunned when I heard he was married. Nash was always the go-it-on-your-own type."

"Love changes things," Ana murmured, and carefully screened all wistfulness from her voice. "Aunt Bryna calls it the purest form of magic."

"A good description. Once it touches you, you begin to think nothing's impossible anymore. Were you ever in love?"

"Once." She looked away, studying the shimmering ice plants along the banks. "A long time ago. But it turned out the magic wasn't strong enough. Then I learned that my life wasn't over after all, and I could be perfectly happy alone. So I bought my house near the water," she said with a smile. "Planted my garden, and started fresh."

"I suppose it was similar for me." He grew thoughtful as they made the final turn toward home. "Does being happy alone mean you don't think you could be happy with someone?"

Unease and hope ran parallel inside her. "I guess it means I can be happy as things stand, until I find someone who not only brings me the magic, but understands it."

He turned into the drive, shut off the engine. "We have something together, Ana."

"I know."

"I never thought to feel anything this powerful again. It's different from what I had before, and I'm not sure what that means. I don't know if I want to know."

"It doesn't matter." She took his hand again. "Sometimes you just have to accept that today is enough."

"No, it's not." He turned to her then, his eyes dark, intense. "Not with you."

She took a careful breath. "I'm not what you think I am, or what you want me to be. Boone—"

"You're exactly what I want." His hands were rough as he dragged her against him. Her startled gasp was muffled against his hard, seeking mouth.

Chapter Ten

A whip of panicked excitement cracked through her as he tore her free of the seat belt and yanked her across his lap. His hands bruised, his mouth branded. This was not the Boone who had loved her so gently, taking her to that sweet, sweet fulfillment with patient hands and murmured promises. Her lover of quiet mornings and lazy afternoons had become something darker, something dangerous, something she was helpless to resist.

She could feel the blood sizzling under her skin as he took those rough, impatient hands over her. This was the wildness she had tasted that first time, in a moonlit garden with the scent of flowers ripe and heady. This bursting of urgent needs was what he had only hinted at under all that patience and steady control.

In mindless acquiescence she strained against him, willing, eager and ready to race along any path he chose.

Her body shuddered once, violently, as he dragged her over a ragged edge. He heard her muffled cry against his greedy mouth, tasted the ripeness of it as her fingers dug desperately into his shoulders. The thought ran crazily through his mind that he could have her here, right here in the car, before reason caught up with either of them.

He tore at her blouse, craving the taste of flesh. The sound of ripping seams was smothered by her quick gasp as he feasted on her throat. Beneath his hungry mouth, her pulse hammered erratically, erotically. The flavor of her was already hot, already honeyed with passion.

On a vicious oath, he shoved the door open, yanking her out. Leaving it swinging, he half carried, half dragged her across the lawn.

"Boone." Staggered, she tried to gain her feet and lost her shoes. "Boone, the car. You left your keys—"

He caught her hair, pulling her head back. His eyes. Oh, Lord, his eyes, she thought, trembling with something much deeper than fear. The heat in them seared through to her soul.

"The hell with the car." His mouth swooped down, plundered hers until she was dazed and dizzy and fighting to breathe. "Do you know what you do to me?" he said between strangled gasps for air. "Every time I see you." He pulled her up the steps, touching her, always touching her. "Soft, serene, with something smoldering just behind your eyes."

He pushed her back against the door, crushing, conquering, those full, luscious lips with his. There was something more in her eyes now. He could see that she was afraid. And that she was aroused. It was as if they both were fully aware that the animal he'd kept ruthlessly on a choke chain for weeks had broken free.

With the breath coming harsh through his lips, he caught her face in his hands. "Tell me. Ana, tell me you want me. Now. My way."

She was afraid she wouldn't be able to speak, her throat was so dry and this new need so huge. "I want you." The husky sound of her voice had the flames in his gut leaping higher. "Now. Any way."

He hooked his hands in her blouse, watched her eyes go to smoke just before he rent it in two. When he kicked the door open, she staggered back, then was caught up in a torrid embrace. Like her blouse, his control was in shreds. His hands tight at her waist, he lifted her off her feet to take her silk-covered breast in his mouth. As crazed now as he, she arched back, her hands fisted in his hair.

"Boone. Please." The plea sobbed out, though she had no idea what she was asking for. Unless it was more.

He lowered her, only so that he could capture her mouth again. His teeth scraped erotically over her swollen lips, his tongue dived deep. Then his heart seemed to explode in his chest as she began to tug frantically at his clothes.

He stumbled toward the stairs, shedding his shirt as he went. Buttons popped and scattered. But his greedy hands reached for her again, yanking the thin chemise down to her waist as they reached the landing.

"Here." He dragged her down with him. "Right here."

At last, he feasted, racing his mouth over her quivering flesh, ruthlessly exploiting her secrets, relentlessly driving her with him where he so desperately needed her to go. No patience here, no rigid control for the sake of her fragility. Indeed, the woman writhing beneath him on the stairs was anything but fragile. There was strength in the hands that gripped him, searing passion in the mouth that tasted him so eagerly, whiplike agility in the body that strained under his.

She felt invincible, immortal, impossibly free. Her body was alive, never more alive, with heat pumping crazily through her blood. The world was spinning around her, a blur of color and blinding lights, whirling faster, faster, until she was forced to grip the pickets of the banister to keep from falling off the edge of the earth.

Her knuckles whitened against the wood as he tore her slacks away, then the thin swatch of lace beneath. His mouth, oh, his mouth, greedy, frantic, fevered. Ana bit back a scream as he sent her flying into hot, airless space.

Her mindless murmurs were in no language he could understand, but he knew he had taken her beyond the boundaries of the sane, of the rational. He wanted her there, right there with him as they catapulted into the madness of vivid, lawless passion.

He'd waited. He'd waited. Now her slim white body bucked. A thoroughbred ready to ride. Quivering like a stallion, he mounted her, driving himself into that wet, waiting heat. She arched to meet him and, hips moving like lightning, raced with him into the roaring dark.

Her hands slid weakly off his damp back. She was too numb to feel the slap of wood against them as they fell against the stairs. She wanted to hold him, but her strength was gone. It wasn't possible to focus her mind on what had happened. All that came were flashes of sensations, bursts of emotions.

If this was the darker side of love, nothing could have prepared her for it. If this terrible need was what had lived inside him, she couldn't comprehend how he could have strapped it back for so long.

For her sake. She turned her damp face into his throat. All for her sake.

Beneath his still-shuddering body, she was as limp as water. Boone struggled to get a grip on reality. He needed to move. After everything else he'd done to her, he was probably crushing her. But when he started to shift, she made a little sound of distress that scraped at his conscience.

"Here, baby, let me help you."

He eased away, picking up a tattered sleeve of her blouse with some idea to cover her. Biting off an oath, he tossed it down again. She'd turned slightly on her side, obviously seeking some kind of comfort. For God's sake, he thought in disgust, he'd taken her like some kind of fiend, and on the stairs. *On the stairs*.

"Ana." He found what was left of his own shirt and tried to wrap it around her shoulders. "Anastasia, I don't know how to explain."

"Explain?" The word was barely audible. Her throat was wild with thirst.

"There's no possible . . . Let me help you up." Her body slid like wax through his arms. "I'll get you some clothes, or . . . Oh, hell."

"I don't think I can get up." She moistened her lips, and tasted him. "Not for a day or two. This is fine, though. I'll just stay right here."

Frowning at her, he tried to interpret what he heard in her voice. It wasn't anger. It didn't sound like distress. It sounded like—very much like—satisfaction. "You're not upset?"

"Hmmm? Am I supposed to be?"

"Well, for . . . I practically attacked you. Hell, I *did* attack you, almost taking you in the front seat of the car, tearing off your clothes, dragging you in here and devouring what was left of you on the stairs."

With her eyes still closed, she drew in a deep breath, then let it out again on a sigh through curved lips. "You certainly did. And it's the first time I've been devoured. I don't think I'll ever go up and down a staircase the same way again."

Gently he tipped a finger under her chin until her eyes opened. "I had intended to at least make it to the bedroom."

"I guess we'll get there eventually." Recognizing concern, she put a hand on his wrist. "Boone, do you think I could be upset because you wanted me that much?"

"I thought you might be upset because this wasn't what you're used to."

Making the effort, she sat up, wincing a little at the aches that would surely be bruises before much longer. "I'm not made of glass. There's no way we could love each other that wouldn't be right. But . . ." She linked her arms around his neck and her smile was wicked around the edges. "Under the circumstances, I'm glad we made it into the house."

He skimmed his hands down to her hips for the pleasure of bringing her body against his. "My neighbor's very open-minded."

"I've heard that." Experimentally she caught his lower lip between her teeth. Remembering how much pleasure it gave her to feel his lips cruise over her face and throat, she began a lazy journey over his. "Fortunately, my neighbor's very understanding of passions. I doubt anything would shock him. Even if I told him I often fantasize about him at night, when I'm alone, in bed."

It was impossible, but he felt himself stir against her. The deep, dark wanting began to smolder again. "Really? What kind of fantasies?"

"Of having him come to me." Her breath began to quicken as his mouth roamed over her shoulder. "Come to my bed like an incubus in the night, when a storm cracks the air. I can see his eyes, cobalt blue in a flash of lightning, and I know that he wants me the way no one else ever has, or ever will."

Knowing very well that if he didn't take some kind of action now they'd remain sprawled on the stairs, he gathered her up. "I can't give you the lightning."

She smiled as he carried her up. "You already have."

Later, hours later, they knelt on the tumbled bed, feasting on pizza by candlelight. Ana had lost track of time and had no need to know if it was midnight or approaching dawn. They had loved and talked and laughed and loved again. No night in her life had been more perfect. What did time matter here?

"Guinevere was no heroine." Ana licked sauce from her fingers. They had discussed epic poetry, modern animation, ancient legends and folklore and classic horror. She wasn't sure how they had wound their way back to Arthur and Camelot, but on the subject of Arthur's queen, Ana stood firm. "And she certainly wasn't a tragic figure."

"I'd think a woman, especially one with your compassion, would have more sympathy with her situation." Boone debated having a last piece from the cardboard box they'd plopped in the center of the bed.

"Why?" Ana picked it up herself and began to feed it to him. "She betrayed her husband, helped bring down a kingdom, all because she was weak-willed and self-indulgent."

"She was in love."

"Love doesn't excuse all actions." Amused, she tilted her head and studied him in the flickering light. He looked gloriously masculine in nothing but a pair of gym shorts, his hair tousled, his face shadowed with stubble. "Isn't that just like a man? Finding excuses for a woman's infidelity just because it's written about in romantic terms."

He didn't think it was precisely an insult, but it made him squirm a little. "I just don't think she had control of the situation."

"Of course she did. She had a choice, and she chose poorly, just as Lancelot did. All that flowery business about gallantry and chivalry and heroism and loyalty, and the two of them justified betraying a man who loved them both because they couldn't control themselves?" She tossed her hair back. "That's bull."

He laughed before he sipped his wine. "You amaze me. Here I've been thinking you were a romantic. A woman who picks flowers by moonlight, who collects statues of faeries and wizards, and she condemns poor Guinevere because she loved unwisely.''

She fired up. ''Poor Guinevere—''

''Hold on.'' He was chuckling, enjoying himself immensely. It didn't occur to either of them that they were debating about people most considered fictional. ''Let's not forget some of the other players. Merlin was supposed to be watching over the whole business. Why didn't he do anything about it?''

Fastidiously she brushed crumbs from her bare legs. ''It's not a sorcerer's place to interfere with destiny.''

''Come on, we're talking about the champ here. One little spell and he could've fixed it up.''

''And altered countless lives,'' she pointed out, gesturing with her glass. ''Skewed history. No, he couldn't do it, not even for Arthur. People—witches, kings, mortals—are responsible for their own fates.''

''He didn't have any problem abetting adultery by disguising Uther as the Duke of Cornwall and taking Tintagel so that Igraine conceived Arthur in the first place.''

''Because that was destiny,'' she said patiently, as she might have to Jessie. ''That was the purpose. For all Merlin's power, all his greatness, his single most vital act was bringing Arthur into being.''

''Sounds like splitting hairs to me.'' He swallowed the last bite of pizza. ''One spell's okay, but another isn't.''

''When you're given a gift, it's your responsibility to know how and when to use it, how and when not to. Can you imagine how he suffered, watching someone he loved destroyed? Knowing, even as Arthur was being conceived, how it would end? Magic doesn't divorce you from emotion or pain. It rarely protects the one who owns it.''

''I guess not.'' He'd certainly had witches and wizards suffering in the stories he wrote. It gave them a human element he found appealing. ''When I was a kid, I used to daydream about living back then.''

''Rescuing fair maidens from fiery dragons?''

''Sure. Going on quests, challenging the Black Knight and beating the hell out of him.''

''Naturally.''

''Then I grew up and discovered I could have the best of both worlds, living there up here—'' he tapped his head with a fingertip ''—when I was writing. And having the creature comforts of the twentieth century.''

''Like pizza.''

''Like pizza,'' he agreed. ''A computer instead of a quill, cotton underwear. Hot running water. Speaking of which...'' he said, fingering the hem of the T-shirt he'd given her to wear. He moved on impulse, and had her shrieking out a laugh as he tossed her over his shoulder and climbed out of bed.

''What are you doing?''

''Hot running water,'' he repeated. ''I think it's time I showed you what I can do in the shower.''

''You're going to sing?''

''Maybe later.'' In the bathroom, he opened the glass shower doors and turned on the taps. ''Hope you like it hot.''

''Well, I—'' She was still over his shoulder when he stepped inside. With the crisscrossing sprays raining, she was immediately drenched, front and back. ''Boone.'' She sputtered. ''You're drowning me.''

"Sorry." He shifted, reaching for the soap. "You know, this shower really sold me on the house. It's roomy." He slicked the wet bar of soap up her calf. "Pretty great having the twin shower heads."

Despite the heat of the water, Ana shivered when he soaped lazy circles at the back of her knee. "It's a little difficult for me to appreciate it from this position." Then she shoved her dripping hair out of her face and noticed that the floor was mirrored tiles. "Oh, my."

He grinned, and moved slowly up to her thigh. "Check out the ceiling."

She did, tilting her head and staring at their reflections. "Ah, doesn't it just steam up?"

"Treated glass. Does get a little foggy if you're in here long enough." And he intended to be in there just long enough. He began sliding her down his body, inch by dangerous inch. "But that only adds to the atmosphere." Gently he pressed her against the back wall, cupping her breasts through the clinging shirt. "Want to hear one of my fantasies?"

"It— Oh." He was rubbing a thumb over an aching nipple. "Seems only fair."

"Better idea." He brushed his lips over hers, teasing, retreating, until her breath began to hitch. "Why don't I show you? First we get rid of this." He dragged the wet shirt over her head, tossing it aside. It landed with a plop that had another tremor jerking through her system. "And I start here." Toying with her mouth, he rubbed the slick soap over her shoulders. "And I don't stop until I get to your toes."

She had a feeling showers were going to join staircases in the more erotic depths of her imagination.

Gripping his hips for balance, she arched back as he circled wet, soapy hands over her breasts.

Steam. It was all around her, it was inside of her. The thick, moist air made it all but impossible to breathe. A tropical storm, water pounding, heat rising. The creamy soap had flesh sliding gloriously against flesh when their bodies moved together. Her hands foamed with it as she ran them over his back, over his chest. Even as his mouth raced to possess, his muscles quivered at her touch, and her laugh was low and softly triumphant.

If she burned, so did he. That was power clashing against power. There was no longer any doubt that she could give back the wild, wanton, wicked pleasure he brought to her. A pleasure so much sweeter, so much richer, because it grew from love, as well as passion.

She wanted to show him. She would show him.

Her hands slid down him, over strong shoulders, the hard chest. She murmured in approval as she traced fingertips over his rib cage and down to the flat plane of his stomach.

He shook his head to try to clear it. He had expected to seduce her here, yet he was being seduced. The delicate hands flowing over his slick skin were shooting arrows of painful need through his system.

"Wait." His hands groped for hers, held them firm. He knew that if she touched him now he would never be able to hold back. "Let me..."

"No." With the new knowledge brimming inside, her mouth seared over his and conquered. "Let me."

Her fingers closed around him, sliding, stroking, squeezing lightly, while his breath sounded harshly in her ear. A fresh flash of triumph exploded inside her as she felt his quick, helpless shudder. Then greed, to have him, all of him, deeply inside her.

"Ana." He felt the last wisps of reality fading. "Ana, I can't—"

"You want me." Delirious with power, she threw her head back. Her eyes were hot with challenge. "Then take me. Now."

She looked like a goddess newly risen from the sea. Wet cables of hair slicked like dark gold over her shoulder. Her skin glowed, shimmered with water. In her eyes were secrets, dark mysteries no man would ever unlock.

She was glorious. She was magnificent. And she was his.

"Hold on to me." Bracing her against the wall, he lifted her hips with his hands. "Hold on to me."

She locked her arms around him, keeping her eyes open. He took her where they stood, plunging into her as the water showered over them. Gasping out his name, she let her head fall back. Through the rising mists, she saw their reflections—a wonderful tangle of limbs that made it impossible to see where he left off and she began.

On a moan of inexpressible pleasure, she dropped her head to his shoulder. She was lost. Lost. Thank God for it. "I love you." She had no idea if the words were in her head or had come through her lips. But she said them again and again until her body convulsed.

He emptied himself into her, then could only stand weakly against the wall as the strength ran out of him. His heart was still roaring in his ears as he closed his hands over her shoulders.

"Tell me now."

Her lips were curved, but she swayed a little and stared up at him through clouded eyes. "Tell you what?"

His fingers tightened, making her eyes clear. "That you love me. Tell me now."

"I... Don't you think we should dry off? We've been in the water quite a while."

With an impatient jerk, he switched off the taps. "I want to look at you when you say it, and have at least some of my wits about me. We're going to stay right here until I hear you say it again."

She hesitated. He could have no idea that he was forcing her to take the next step toward having him— or losing him. Destiny, she thought, and choices. It was time she made hers. "I love you. I wouldn't be here with you, couldn't be here, if I didn't."

His eyes were very dark, very intense. Slowly his grip lightened, his face relaxed. "I feel as though I've waited years to hear you say that."

She brushed the wet hair away from his brow. "You only had to ask."

He caught her hands in his. "You don't." Because she was beginning to shiver, he drew her out of the stall to wrap her in a towel. He caught it close around her, then wrapped his arms tight for more warmth. "Anastasia." Tenderness swelled inside him as he touched his lips to her hair, her cheek, her mouth. "You don't have to ask. I love you. You brought something I thought I'd never have again, never want again, back into my life."

On a broken sigh, she pressed her face to his chest. This was real, she thought. This was hers. She would find a way to keep it. "You're everything I've ever wanted. Don't stop loving me, Boone. Don't stop."

"I couldn't." He drew her away. "Don't cry."

"I don't." The tears shimmered, but didn't spill over. "I don't cry."

Anastasia sheds no tears, but she'll shed them for you.

Sebastian's words rang uncomfortably in Boone's head. Resolutely he blocked them out. It was ridiculous. He'd do nothing to hurt her. He opened his mouth, then closed it again. A steamy bathroom was no place for the proposal he wanted to make. And there were things he needed to tell her first.

"Let's get you another shirt. We need to talk."

She was much too happy to pay any heed to the curl of uneasiness. She laughed when he took her back to the bedroom and tugged another of his shirts over her head. Dreamily she poured two more glasses of wine while he pulled on a pair of jeans.

"Will you come with me?" He held out a hand, and she took it willingly.

"Where are we going?"

"I want to show you something." He took her down the shadowy hall, into his office. Delighted, Ana turned a circle.

"This is where you work."

There were wide, uncurtained windows framed with curving cherrywood. A couple of worn, faded scatter rugs had been tossed on the hardwood floor. Starshine sprinkled through the twin skylights. An industrious-looking computer, reams of paper and shelves of books announced that this was a workplace. But he'd added charm with framed illustrations, a collection of dragons and knights that intrigued her. The winged faery he'd bought from Morgana had a prominent place on a high, carved stool.

"You need some plants," she decided instantly, thinking of the narcissus and daffodils she was forcing in her greenhouse. "I imagine you spend hours in this room every day." She glanced down at the empty ashtray beside his machine.

Following her gaze, he frowned. Odd, he thought, he hadn't had a cigarette in days—had forgotten about them completely. He'd have to congratulate himself later.

"Sometimes I watch out the window when you're in your garden. It makes it difficult to concentrate."

She laughed and sat on the corner of his desk. "We'll get you some shades."

"Not a chance." He smiled, but his hands went nervously to his pockets. "Ana, I need to tell you about Alice."

"Boone." Compassion had her rising again to reach out. "I understand. I know it's painful. There's no need to explain anything to me"

"There is for me." With her hand in his, he turned to gesture at a sketch on the wall. A lovely young girl was kneeling by a stream, dipping a golden pail into the silver water. "She drew that, before Jessie was born. Gave it to me for our first anniversary."

"It's beautiful. She was very talented."

"Yeah. Very talented, very special." He sipped his wine in an unconscious toast to a lost love. "I knew her most of my life. Pretty Alice Reeder."

He needed to talk, Ana thought. She would listen. "You were high school sweethearts?"

"No." He laughed at that. "Not even close. Alice was a cheerleader, student body president, all-around nice girl who always made the honor roll. We ran in different crowds, and she was a couple of years behind me. I was going through my obligatory rebellious period and kind of hulked around school, looking tough.''

She smiled, touched his cheek where the stubble was rough. ''I'd like to have seen that.''

''I snuck cigarettes in the bathroom, and Alice painted scenery for school plays. We knew each other, but that was about it. I went off to college, ended up in New York. It seemed necessary, since I was going to write, that I get myself a loft and starve a little.''

She slipped an arm around him, instinctively offering comfort, waiting while he gathered his thoughts.

''One morning I was in the bakery around the corner from where I was living, and I looked up from the crullers and there she was, buying coffee and a croissant. We started talking. You know... what are you doing here, the old neighborhood, what had happened to whom. That kind of thing. It was comforting, and exciting. Here we were, two small-town kids taking on big bad New York.''

And fate had tossed them together, Ana thought, in a city of millions.

''She was in art school,'' Boone continued, ''sharing an apartment only a couple of blocks away with some other girls. I walked her to the subway. We just sort of drifted together, sitting in the park, comparing sketches, talking for hours. Alice was so full of life, energy, ideas. We didn't fall in love so much as we slid into it.'' His eyes softened as he studied the sketch. ''Very slowly, very sweetly. We got married just before I sold my first book. She was still in college.''

He had to stop again as the memories swam back in force. Instinctively his hand closed over Ana's. She opened herself, giving what strength and support she could.

"Anyway, everything seemed so perfect. We were young, happy, in love. She'd already been commissioned to do a painting. We found out she was pregnant. So we decided to move back home, raise the child in a nice suburban atmosphere close to family. Then Jessie came, and it seemed as though nothing could ever go wrong. Except that Alice never seemed to really get her energy back after the birth. Everyone said it was natural, she was bound to be tired with a new baby and her work. She lost weight. I used to joke that she was going to fade away." He closed his eyes for a minute. "That's just what she did. She faded away. When it had gone on long enough for us to worry, she had tests, but there was a mess-up in the lab and they didn't detect it soon enough. By the time we found out she had cancer, it was too late to stop it."

"Oh, Boone. I'm sorry. I'm so sorry."

"She suffered. That was the worst. She suffered and there was nothing I could do. I watched her die, degree by degree. And I thought I would die, too. But there was Jessie. Alice was only twenty-five when I buried her. Jessie had just turned two." He took a long breath before he turned to Ana. "I loved Alice. I always will."

"I know. When someone touches your life that way, you never lose it."

"When I lost her, I stopped believing in happy-ever-after, except in books. I didn't want to fall in love again, risk that kind of pain—for myself or for Jessie. But I have fallen in love again. What I feel for you is so strong, it makes me believe again. It's not the same as I felt before. It's not less. It's just . . . us."

She touched his cheek. She thought she understood. "Boone, did you think I would ask you to forget her? That I could resent or be jealous of what you had with her? It only makes me love you more. She made you happy. She gave you Jessie. I only wish I had known her."

Impossibly moved, he lowered his brow to hers. "Marry me, Ana."

Chapter Eleven

She froze. The hands that had reached up to bring him close stopped in midair. Her breath seemed to stall in her lungs. Even as her heart leapt with hope, her mind warned her to wait.

Very slowly, she eased out of his arms. "Boone, I think—"

"Don't tell me I'm rushing things." He was amazingly calm now that he'd taken the step—the step he realized he'd already taken in his head weeks before. "I don't care if I'm moving too fast. I need you in my life, Ana."

"I'm already in your life." She smiled, trying to keep it light. "I told you that."

"It was hard enough when I only wanted you, harder still when I started to care. But it's impossible now that I'm in love with you. I don't want to live next door to you." He took a firm grip on her shoulders to keep her still. "I don't want to have to send my child away so I can spend the night with you. You said you loved me."

"I do." She gave in to desperate need and pressed herself against him. "You know I do, more than I thought I could. More than I wanted to. But marriage is—"

"Right." He stroked a hand down her damp hair. "Right for us. Ana, I told you once I don't take intimacy lightly, and I wasn't just talking about sex." He drew her back, wanting to see her face, wanting her to see his. "I'm talking about what's inside me every time I look at you. Before I met you, I was content to keep my life the way it was. But that's no good anymore. I'm not going to keep running through the hedges to be with you. I want you with me, with us."

"Boone, if it could be so simple." She turned away, struggling to find the right answer.

"It can be." He fought against a quick flutter of panic. "When I walked in this morning and saw you in bed, with your arms around Jessie—I can't tell you what went through me at that moment. I realized that was what I wanted. For you to be there. Just to be there. To know I could share her with you, because you'd love her. That there could be other children. A future."

She shut her eyes, because the image was so sweet, so perfect. And she was denying them both a chance to make the image reality, because she was afraid. "If I said yes now, before you understand me, before you know me, it wouldn't be fair."

"I do know you." He swept her around again. "I know you have passion, and compassion, that you're loyal and generous and openhearted. That you have strong feelings for family, that you like romantic music and apple wine. I know the way your laugh sounds, the way you smell. And I know that I could make you happy, if you'd let me."

"You do make me happy. It's because I don't want to do any less for you that I don't know what to do." She broke away to walk off the tension. "I didn't know this was going to happen so quickly, before I was sure. I swear, if I'd known you were thinking of marriage..."

To be his wife, she thought. Bound to him by handfast. She could think of nothing more precious than that kind of belonging.

She had to tell him, so that he would have the choice of accepting or backing away. "You've been much more honest with me than I with you."

"About?"

"About what you are." Her eyes closed on a sigh. "I'm a coward. So easily devastated by bad feelings, afraid, pathetically afraid, of pain—physical and emotional. So hatefully vulnerable to what others can be indifferent to."

"I don't know what you're talking about, Ana."

"No, you don't." She pressed her lips together. "Can you understand that there are some who are more sensitive than others to strong feelings? Some who have to develop a defense against absorbing too much of the swirl of emotion that goes on around them? Who have to, Boone, because they couldn't survive otherwise?"

He pushed back his impatience and tried to smile. "Are you getting mystical on me?"

She laughed, pressing a hand to her eyes. "You don't know the half of it. I need to explain, and don't know how. If I could—" She started to turn back, determined to tell him everything, and the sketchpad on his desk slid off at the movement. Automatically she bent to pick it up.

Perhaps it was fate that it had fallen faceup, showing a recently completed sketch. An excellent one, Ana thought on a long breath as she studied it. The fierce and wicked lines of the black-caped witch glared up at her. Evil, she thought. He had captured evil perfectly.

"Don't worry about that." He started to take it from her, but she shook her head.

"Is this for your story?"

"*The Silver Castle,* yes. Let's not change the subject."

"Not as much as you think," she murmured. "Indulge me a minute," she said with a careful smile. "Tell me about the sketch."

"Damn it, Ana."

"Please."

Frustrated, he dragged a hand through his hair. "It's just what it looks like. The evil witch who put the spell on the princess and the castle. I had to figure there was a spell that kept anyone from getting in or out."

"So you chose a witch."

"I know it's obvious. But the story seemed to call for it. The vindictive, jealous witch, furious with the princess's goodness and beauty, casts the spell, so the princess stays trapped inside, cut off from love and life and happiness. Then, when true love conquers, the spell's broken and the witch is vanquished. And they live happily ever after.''

"I suppose witches are, to you, evil and calculating." Calculating, she remembered. It was one of the words Robert had tossed at her. That, and much, much worse.

"Goes with the territory. Power corrupts, right?''

She set the sketch aside. "There are those who think it." It was only a drawing, she told herself. Only part of a story he'd created. Yet it served to remind her how large a span they needed to cross. "Boone, I'll ask you for something tonight."

"I guess you could ask me for anything tonight."

"Time," she said. "And faith. I love you, Boone, and there's no one else I'd want to spend my life with. But I need time, and so do you. A week," she said before he could protest. "Only a week. Until the full moon. Then there are things I'll tell you. After I do, I hope you'll ask me again to be your wife. If you do, if you can, then I'll say yes."

"Say yes now." He caught her close, capturing her mouth, hoping he could persuade her by his will alone. "What difference will a week make?''

"All," she whispered, clinging tight. "Or none."

He didn't care to wait. It made him nervous and impatient that the days seemed to crawl by. One, then two, finally three. To comfort himself, he thought about the turn his life would take once the interminable week was over.

No more nights alone. Soon, when he returned restlessly in the dark, she would be there. The house would be full of her, her scent, the fragrances of her herbs and oils. On those long, quiet evenings, they could sit together on the deck and talk about the day, about tomorrows.

Or perhaps she would want them to move into her house. It wouldn't matter. They could walk through her gardens, under her arbors, and she could try to teach him the names of all of her flowers.

They could take a trip to Ireland, and she could show him all the important places of her childhood. There would be stories she could tell him, like the one about the witch and the frog, and he could write about them.

One day there would be more children, and he would see her holding their baby the way she had held Morgana and Nash's.

More children. That thought brought him up short and had him staring at the framed picture of Jessie smiling out at him from his desktop.

His baby. Only his, and his only, for so long now. He did want more children. He'd never realized until now how much he wanted more. How much he enjoyed being a father. It was simply something he was, something he did.

Now as his mind began to play with the idea, he could see himself soothing an infant in the night as he had once soothed Jessie. Holding out his arms as a toddler took those first shaky steps. Tossing a ball in the yard, holding on to the back of an unsteady bike.

A son. Wouldn't it be incredible to have a son? Or another daughter. Brothers and sisters for Jessie. She'd love that, he thought, and found himself grinning like an idiot. He'd love it.

Of course, he hadn't even asked Ana how she felt about adding to the family. That was certainly something they'd have to discuss. Maybe it would be rushing her again to bring it up now.

Then he remembered how she'd looked with her arm cuddling Jessie in his bed. The way her face had glowed when she'd held two tiny infants up so that his daughter could see and touch.

No, he decided. He knew her. She would be as anxious as he to turn their love into life.

By the end of the week, he thought, they would start making plans for their future together.

For Ana, the days passed much too quickly. She spent hours going over the right way to tell Boone everything. Then she would change her mind and struggle to think of another way.

There was the brash way.

She imagined herself sitting him down in her kitchen with a pot of tea between them. "Boone," she would say, "I'm a witch. If that doesn't bother you, we can start planning the wedding."

There was the subtle way.

They would sit out on her patio, near the arbor of morning glories. While they sipped wine and watched the sunset, they would talk about their childhoods.

"Growing up in Ireland is a little different than growing up in Indiana, I suppose," she would tell him. "But the Irish usually take having witches in the neighborhood pretty much for granted." Then she'd smile. "More wine, love?"

Or the intellectual way.

"I'm sure you'd agree most legends have some basis in fact." This conversation would take place on the beach, with the sound of the surf and the cry of gulls. "Your books show a great depth of understanding and respect for what most consider myth or folklore. Being a witch myself, I appreciate your positive slant on faeries and magic. Particularly the way you handled the enchantress in *A Third Wish for Miranda.*"

Ana only wished she had enough humor left to laugh at each pitiful scenario. She was certainly going to have to think of something, now that she had less than twenty-four hours to go.

Boone had already been more patient than she had a right to ask. There was no excuse for keeping him waiting any longer.

At least she would have some moral support this evening. Morgana and Sebastian and their spouses were on their way over for the monthly Friday-night cookout. If that didn't buck her up for her confrontation with Boone the following day, nothing would. As she stepped onto the patio, she fingered the diamond-clear zircon she wore around her neck.

Obviously Jessie had been keeping an eagle eye out, for she zipped through the hedge, with Daisy yipping behind her. To show his indifference to the pup, Quigley sat down and began to wash his hindquarters.

"We're coming to your house for a cookout," Jessie announced. "The babies are coming, too, and maybe I can hold one. If I'm really, really careful."

"I think that could be arranged." Automatically Ana scanned the neighboring yard for signs of Boone. "How was school today, sunshine?"

"It was pretty neat. I can write my name, and Daddy's and yours. Yours is easiest. I can write Daisy's, but I don't know how to spell Quigley's, so I just wrote *cat*. Then I had my whole family, just like the teacher told us." She stopped, scuffed her shoes, and for the first time since Ana had known her, looked shy. "Was it okay if I said you were my family?"

"It's more than okay." Crouching down, Ana gave Jessie a huge hug. Oh, yes, she thought, squeezing her eyes tight. This is what I want, what I need. I could be a wife to him, a mother to the child. Please, please, let me find the way to have it all. "I love you, Jessie."

"You won't go away, will you?"

Because they were close, because she couldn't prevent it, Ana touched the child's heart and understood that Jessie was thinking of her mother. "No, baby." She drew back, choosing her words with care. "I would never want to go away. But if I had to, if I couldn't help it, I'd still be close."

"How can you go away and still be close?"

"Because I'd keep you in my heart. Here." Ana took the thin braided gold chain with the square of zircon and slipped it over Jessie's neck.

"Ooh! It shines!"

"It's very special. When you feel lonely or sad, you hold on to this and think of me. I'll know, and I'll send you happiness."

Dazzled, Jessie turned the crystal, and it exploded with light and color. "Is it magic?"

"Yes."

Jessie accepted the answer with a child's faith. "I want to show Daddy." She started to dash off, then remembered her manners. "Thank you."

"You're welcome. Is— Ah, is Boone inside?"

"Uh-uh, he's on the roof."

"The roof?"

"'Cause next month is Christmas, and he's starting to put up the lights so we know how many we have
to buy. The whole house is going to be lit up. Daddy
says this is going to be the most special Christmas
ever."

"I hope so." Ana shielded her eyes with the flat of
her hand and looked up. There he was, sitting on top
of the house, looking back at her. Her heart gave that
quick, improbable leap it always did when she saw
him. Despite nerves, she smiled, lifting one hand in a
wave while the other rested on Jessie's shoulder.

It would be all right, she told herself. It had to be.

Boone ignored the tangle of Christmas lights beside him and pleased himself by watching them until
Jessie raced back across the yard and Ana went inside.

It would be all right, he told himself. It had to be.

Sebastian plucked a fat black olive from a tray and
popped it into his mouth. "When do we eat?"

"You already are," Mel pointed out.

"I mean real food." He winked down at Jessie.
"Hot dogs."

"Herbed chicken," Ana corrected, turning a sizzling thigh on the grill.

They were spread over the patio, with Jessie sitting
in a wrought-iron chair carefully cradling a cooing
Allysia in her lap. Boone and Nash were deep in a dis-
cussion on infant care. Morgana had Donovan at her
breast, comfortably nursing, while she listened to Mel

relate the happy ending of the runaway she and Sebastian had tracked down.

"Kid was miserable," she was saying. "Sorry as hell he'd taken off, scared to go back. When we found him—cold, broke and hungry—and he realized his parents were scared instead of angry, he couldn't wait to get home. I think he's grounded till he's thirty, but he doesn't seem to care." She waited until Morgana had burped her son. Her hands had been itching to touch. "Want me to put him back down for you?"

"Thanks." Morgana watched Mel's face as she lifted the baby. "Thinking about having one of your own. Or two?"

"Actually." Mel caught the special scent of baby and felt her knees go weak. "I think I might..." She cast a quick look over her shoulder and saw her husband was busy teasing Jessie. "I'm not sure yet, but I think I may have already started."

"Oh, Mel, that's—"

"Shh." She leaned down, using the baby for cover. "I don't want him to know, or even suspect, or I'd never be able to stop him from looking for himself. I want to be able to tell him about this." She grinned. "It'll knock his socks off."

Gently Mel laid the child in his side of the double carriage.

"Allysia's sleeping too," Jessie pointed out, tracing a finger over the baby's cheek.

"Want to put her down with her brother?" Sebastian leaned over to help Jessie stand with the baby. "That's the way." He kept his hands under hers as she laid Allysia down. "You'll be an excellent mother one day."

"Maybe I can have twins, too." She turned when Daisy began to bark. "Hush," she whispered. "You'll wake the babies."

But Daisy was lost in the thrill of the chase. Heading for open ground, Quigley shot through the hedges into the next yard, yowling. Delighted with the game, Daisy dashed after him.

"I'll get him, Daddy." Making as much racket as the animals, Jessie raced after them.

"I don't think obedience school's the answer," Boone commented, tipping back a beer. "I'm thinking along the lines of a mental institution."

Panting a bit, Jessie followed the sounds of barks and hisses, across the yard, over the deck, around the side of the house. When she caught up with Daisy, she put her hands on her hips and scolded.

"You have to be friends. Ana won't like it if you keep teasing Quigley."

Daisy simply thumped her tail on the ground and barked again. Halfway up the ladder Boone had used to climb to the roof, Quigley hissed and spat.

"He doesn't like it, Daisy." On a sigh, she squatted down to pet the dog. "He doesn't know you're just playing and wouldn't really hurt him ever. You made him scared." She looked up the ladder. "Come on, kitty. It's okay. You can come down now."

On a feline growl, Quigley narrowed his eyes, then bounded up the ladder when Daisy responded with another flurry of barks.

"Oh, Daisy, look what you've done." Jessie hesitated at the foot of the ladder. Her father had been very specific about her not going near it. But he hadn't known that Quigley would get so scared. And maybe he'd fall off the roof and get killed. She stepped back, thinking she would go tell her father to come. Then she heard Quigley meow.

Daisy was her responsibility, she remembered. She was supposed to feed him and watch him so he didn't get in trouble. If Quigley got hurt, it would be all her fault.

"I'm coming, kitty. Don't be scared." With her lower lip caught between her teeth, she started up the rungs. She'd seen her father go right on up, and it hadn't looked hard at all. Just like climbing the jungle gyms at school, or up to the top of the big sliding board. "Kitty, kitty," she chanted, climbing higher and giggling when Quigley stuck his head over the roof. "You silly cat, Daisy was only playing. I'll take you down, don't worry."

She was nearly to the top when her sneakered foot missed the next rung.

"Smells wonderful," Boone murmured, but he was sniffing at Ana's neck, not the chicken she'd piled on a platter. "Good enough to eat."

Nash gave him a nudge as he reached for a plate. "If you're going to kiss her, move aside. The rest of us want dinner."

"Fine." Slipping his arms around a flustered Ana, he closed his mouth over hers in a long, lingering kiss. "Time's almost up," he said against her mouth. "You could put me out of my misery now, and—"

The words shut off when he heard Jessie's scream. With his heart in his throat, he raced across the yard, shouting for her. He tore through the hedges, pounded across the grass.

"Oh, God! Oh, my God!"

Every ounce of blood seemed to drain out of him when he saw her crumpled on the ground, her arm bent at an impossible angle, her face as white as linen.

"Baby!" Panicked, he fell beside her. She was too still—even his fevered mind registered that one terrifying fact. And when he reached down to pick her up, there was blood, her blood, on his hands.

"Don't move her!" Ana snapped out the order as she dropped beside them. She was breathing hard, fighting back terror, but her hands clasped firmly over his wrists. "You don't know how or where she's hurt. You can do more harm by moving her."

"She's bleeding." He cupped his hands on his daughter's face. "Jessie. Come on, Jessie." With a trembling finger, he searched for a pulse at her throat. "Don't do this. Dear God, don't do this. We need an ambulance."

"I'll call," Mel said from behind them.

Ana only shook her head. "Boone." The calm settled over her as she understood what she had to do. "Boone, listen to me." She took his shoulders, holding tight when he tried to shake her off. "You have to move back. Let me look at her. Let me help her."

"She's not breathing." He could only stare down at his little girl. "I don't think she's breathing. Her arm. She's broken her arm."

It was more than that. Even without a closer link, Ana knew it was much more than that. And there was no time for an ambulance. "I can help her, but you have to move back."

"She needs a doctor. For God's sake, someone call an ambulance."

"Sebastian," Ana said quietly. Her cousin stepped forward and took Boone's arms.

"Let go of me!" Boone started to swing and found himself pinned by both Sebastian and Nash. "What the hell's wrong with you? We have to get her to a hospital!"

"Let Ana do what she can," Nash said, fighting to hold his friend and his own panic back. "You have to trust her, for Jessie's sake."

"Ana." Pale and shaken, Morgana passed one of her babies into Mel's waiting arms. "It may be too late. You know what could happen to you if—"

"I have to try."

Very gently, oh, so gently, she placed her hands on either side of Jessie's head. She braced, waiting until her own breathing was slow and deep. It was hard, very hard, to block out Boone's violent and terrified emotions, but she focused on the child, only the child. And opened herself.

Pain. Hot, burning spears of it, radiating through her head. Too much pain for such a small child. Ana drew it out, drew it in, let her own system absorb it. When agony threatened to smother the serenity needed for such deep and delicate work, she waited for it to roll past. Then moved on.

So much damage, she thought as her hands trailed lightly down. Such a long way to fall. A perfect image clicked in her mind. The ground rushing up, the help-less fear, the sudden, numbing jolt of impact.

Her fingers passed over a deep gash in Jessie's shoulder. The mirror image sliced through her own, throbbed, seeped blood. Then both slowly faded.

"My God." Boone stopped struggling. His body was too numb. "What is she doing? How?"

"She needs quiet," Sebastian muttered. Stepping back from Boone, he took Morgana's hand. There was nothing they could do but wait.

The injuries inside were severe. Sweat began to bloom on Ana's skin as she examined, absorbed, mended. She was chanting as she worked, knowing she needed to deepen the trance to save the child, and herself.

Oh, but the pain! It ripped through her like fire, making her shudder. Her breath hitched as she fought the need to pull back. Blindly she clutched a hand over the zircon Jessie still wore and placed the other over the child's quiet heart.

When she threw her head back, her eyes were the color of storm clouds, and as blank as glass.

The light was bright, blindingly bright. She could barely see the child up ahead. She called, shouted, wanting to hurry, knowing that one misstep now would end it for both of them.

She stared into the light and felt Jessie slipping further away.

"This gift is mine to use or scorn." Both pain and power shimmered in her voice. "This choice was mine from the day I was born. What harms the child bring into me. As I will, so mote it be."

She cried out then, from the tearing price to be paid for cheating death. She felt her own life ebb, teetering, teetering toward the searing light as Jessie's heart began to beat tremulously under her hand.

She fought back, for both of them, calling on every ounce of her strength, every vestige of her power.

Boone saw his daughter stir, watched her lashes flutter as Ana swayed back.

"Jess—Jessie?" He leaped forward to scoop her into his arms. "Baby, are you all right?"

"Daddy?" Her blank, unfocused eyes began to clear. "Did I fall down?"

"Yeah." Weak with relief and gratitude, he buried his face against her throat and rocked her. "Yeah."

"Don't cry, Daddy." She patted his back. "I'm okay."

"Let's see." He took a shaky breath before he ran his hands over her. There was no blood, he discovered. No blood, no bruise, not even the smallest scratch. He held her close again, staring at Ana as Sebastian helped her to her feet. "Do you hurt anywhere, Jessie?"

"Uh-uh." She yawned and nestled her head on his shoulder. "I was going to Mommy. She looked so pretty in all the light. But she looked sad, like she was going to cry, when she saw me coming. Then Ana was there, and she took my hand. Mommy looked happy when she waved goodbye to us. I'm sleepy, Daddy."

His own heart was throbbing in his throat, thickening his voice. "Okay, baby."

"Why don't you let me take her up?" When Boone hesitated, Nash lowered his voice. "She's fine. Ana's not." He took the already dozing child. "Don't let common sense get in the way, pal," he added as he took Jessie inside.

"I want to know what happened here." Afraid he'd babble, Boone forced himself to speak slowly. "I want to know exactly what happened."

"All right." Ana glanced around at her family. "If you'd leave us alone for just a minute, I'd like to..." She trailed off as the world went gray. Swearing, Boone caught her as she fell, then hoisted her into his arms.

"What the hell is going on?" he demanded. "What did she do to Jessie?" He looked down, alarmed by the translucent pallor of Ana's cheeks. "What did she do to herself?"

"She saved your daughter's life," Sebastian said. "And risked her own."

"Be quiet, Sebastian," Morgana murmured. "He's been through enough."

"He?"

"Yes." She laid a restraining hand on her cousin's arm. "Boone, Ana needs rest, a great deal of rest and quiet. If you'd prefer, you can bring her home. One of us will stay and take care of her."

"She'll stay here." He turned and carried her inside.

She was drifting in and out, in and out of worlds without color. There was no pain now, no feeling at all. She was as insubstantial as a mist. Once or twice she heard Sebastian or Morgana slip inside her deeply sleeping mind to offer reassurance. Others joined them, her parents, her aunts and uncles, and more.

After a long, long journey, she felt herself coming back. Tints and hues seeped back into the colorless world. Sensations began to prickle along her skin. She sighed once—it was the first sound she had made in more than twenty-four hours—then opened her eyes.

Boone watched her come back. He rose automatically from the chair to bring her the medication Morgana had left with him.

"Here." He supported her, holding the cup to her lips. "You're supposed to drink this."

She obeyed, recognizing the scent and the taste. "Jessie?"

"She's fine. Nash and Morgana picked her up this afternoon. She's staying with them tonight."

With a nod, she drank again. "How long have I been asleep?"

"Asleep?" He gave a half laugh at her prosaic term for the comalike state she'd been in. "You've been out for twenty-six hours." He glanced at his watch. "And thirty minutes."

The longest journey she'd ever taken, Ana realized. "I need to call my family and tell them I'm well."

"I'll do it. Are you hungry?"

"No." She tried not to be hurt by his polite, distant tone of voice. "This is all I need for now."

"Then I'll be back in a minute."

When he left her alone, she covered her face with her hands. Her own fault, she berated herself. She hadn't prepared him, had dragged her feet, and fate had taken a hand. On a tired sigh, she got out of bed and began to dress.

"What the hell are you doing?" Boone demanded when he walked in again. "You're supposed to rest."

"I've rested enough." Ana stared down at her hands as she meticulously buttoned her blouse. "And I'd just as soon be on my feet when we talk about this."

His nerves jittered, but he only nodded. "Have it your way."

"Can we go outside? I could use some air."

"Fine." He took her arm and led her downstairs and out on the deck. Once she was seated, he took out a cigarette, struck a match. He'd hardly closed his eyes since he'd carried Ana upstairs, and he'd been subsisting on tobacco and coffee. "If you're feeling up to it, I'd appreciate an explanation."

"I'm going to try to give you one. I'm sorry I didn't tell you before." Ana linked her hands tight in her lap. "I wanted to, but I could never find the right way."

"Straight out," he said as he dragged deeply on smoke.

"I come from a very old bloodline—on both sides. A different culture, if you like. Do you know what wicca is?"

Something cold brushed his skin, but it was only the night air. "Witchcraft."

"Actually, its true meaning is wise. But witch will do." She looked up, and her clear gray eyes met his tired, shadowed ones. "I'm a hereditary witch, born with empathic powers that enable me to link emotionally, and physically, with others. My gift is one of healing."

Boone took another long drag on his cigarette. "You're going to sit there, look me in the face and tell me you're a witch."

"Yes."

Furious, he flung the cigarette away. "What kind of a game is this, Ana? Don't you think after what happened here last night I deserve a reasonable explanation?"

"I think you deserve the truth. You may not think it reasonable." She held up a hand before he could speak. "Tell me how you would explain what happened."

He opened his mouth, closed it again. He'd been working on that single problem for more than twenty-four hours without finding a comfortable solution. "I can't. But that doesn't mean I'm going to buy into this."

"All right." She rose, laid a hand on his chest. "You're tired. You haven't had much sleep. Your head's pounding and your stomach's in knots."

He lifted a brow derisively. "I don't think you have to be a witch to figure that out."

"No." Before he could back away, she touched a hand to his brow, pressed the other to his stomach. "Better?" she asked after a moment.

He needed to sit down, but he was afraid he wouldn't get up again. She'd touched him, barely touched him. And even the shadow of pain was gone. "What is it? Hypnotism?"

"No. Boone, look at me."

He did, and saw a stranger with tangled blond hair billowing out in the wind. The amber enchantress, he thought numbly. Was it any wonder it had reminded him so much of her?

Ana saw both shock and the beginning of belief on his face. "When you asked me to marry you, I asked you to give me time so that I could find the right way to tell you. I was afraid." Her hands dropped away. "Afraid you'd look at me exactly the way you're looking at me now. As if you don't even know me."

"This is bull. Look, I write this stuff for a living, and I know fiction from fact."

"My skill for magic is very limited." Still, she reached into her pocket, where she always carried a few crystals. With her eyes on Boone's, she held them out in her palm. Slowly they began to glow, the purple of the amethyst deepening, the pink of the rose quartz brightening, the green of the malachite shimmering. Then they rose, an inch, two inches, up, circling, spinning in the air and flashing with light. "Morgana is more talented with such things."

He stared at the tumbling crystals, trying to find a logical reason. "Morgana is a witch, too?"

"She's my cousin," Ana said simply.

"Which makes Sebastian—"

"Sebastian's gift is sight."

He didn't want to believe, but it was impossible to discount what he saw with his own eyes. "Your family," he began. "Those magic tricks of your father's."

"Magic in its purest form." She plucked the crystals out of the air and slipped them back in her pocket. "As I told you, he's very accomplished. As are the rest of them, in their own ways. We're witches. All of us." She reached out to him, but he backed away. "I'm sorry."

"You're sorry?" Rocked to the core, he dragged both hands through his hair. It had to be a dream, a nightmare. But he was standing on his own deck, feeling the wind, hearing the sea. "That's good. That's great. You're sorry. For what, Ana? For being what you are, or for not finding it important enough to mention?"

"I'm not sorry for being what I am." Pride stiffened her spine. "I am sorry for making excuses to myself not to tell you. And I'm sorry, most sorry of all, that you can't look at me now the way you did only a day ago."

"What do you expect? Am I supposed to just shrug this off, pick up where we were before? To accept the fact that the woman I love is something out of one of my own stories, and think nothing of it?"

"I'm exactly what I was yesterday, and what I'll be tomorrow."

"A witch."

"Yes." She folded her hands at her waist. "A witch, born to the craft. I don't make poisoned apples or lure children into houses of gingerbread."

"That's supposed to relieve my mind?"

"Even I don't have the power to do that. As I told you, all of us are responsible for our own destinies." But she knew he held hers in his hands. "You have your choice to make."

He struggled to get a grip on it, and simply couldn't. "You needed time to tell me. Well, by God, I need time to figure out what to do about it." He started to pace, then stopped dead. "Jessie. Jessie's over at Morgana's."

Ana felt the crack in her heart widen. "Oh, yes, with my cousin the witch." A single tear spilled over and ran down her cheek. "What do you think Morgana's going to do? Cast a spell on her? Lock her in a tower?"

"I don't know what to think. For Lord's sake, I've found myself in the middle of a fairy tale! What am I supposed to think?"

"What you will," Ana said wearily. "I can't change what I am, and I wouldn't. Not even for you. And I won't stand here and have you look at me as if I were a freak.''

"I'm not—"

"Shall I tell you what you're feeling?" she asked him as another tear fell. "Betrayed, angry, hurt. And suspicious of what I am, what I can do, or will do."

"My feelings are my own business," he shot back, shaken. "I don't want you to get inside me that way."

"I know. And if I were to step forward right now, reach out to you as a woman, you'd only back away. So I'll save us both. Good night, Boone."

When she walked off the deck, into the shadows, he couldn't bring himself to call her back.

Chapter Twelve

"I guess you're still a little dazed." Nash lounged against the rail of Boone's deck, enjoying a beer and the cool evening breeze.

"I was never a *little* dazed," Boone told him. "Look, maybe I'm just a narrow-minded sort of guy, Nash, but finding out the lady next door is a witch kind of threw me off stride."

"Especially when you're in love with the lady next door."

"Especially. I wouldn't have believed it. Who would? But I saw what she did with Jessie. Then I started piecing other things together." He laughed shortly. "Sometimes I still wake up in the middle of the night and think I dreamed the whole thing." He walked over to the rail, leaning out toward the sound of water. "It shouldn't be real. She shouldn't be real."

"Why not? Come on, Boone, it's our business to stretch the envelope a little."

"This blows the envelope wide open," Boone pointed out. "And what we do, we do for books, for movies. It's entertainment, Nash, it's not life."

"It's mine now."

Boone blew out a breath. "I guess it is. But didn't you...don't you even question it, or worry about it?"

"Sure, I did. I thought she was pulling my leg until she tossed me up in the air and left me hanging there." The memory made him grin, even as Boone shut his eyes. "Morgana's not the subtle type. Once I realized the whole thing was on the level, it was wild, you know?"

"Wild," Boone repeated.

"Yeah. I mean, I've spent most of my life making up stories about this kind of thing, and here I end up marrying an honest-to-goodness witch. Elfin blood and everything."

"Elfin blood." The term had Boone's head reeling. "It doesn't bother you?"

"Why should it bother me? It makes her who she is, and I love her. I have to admit I'm a little dubious about the kids. I mean, once they get going, I'll be outnumbered."

"The twins." Boone had to force his mouth to close. "Are you telling me those babies are...will be..."

"A pretty sure bet. Come on, Boone, they aren't going to grow warts and start to cackle. They just get a little something extra. Mel's expecting, too. She just found out for sure. She's the most down-to-earth lady

I know. And she's handling Sebastian as if she's been around a psychic all her life.''

"So you're saying, 'Loosen up, Boone. What's your problem?'''

Nash dropped down on the bench. "I know it's not that easy.''

"Let me ask you this.... How far into the relationship were you when Morgana told you about her—what do I call it?—her heritage.''

"Pretty much right off the bat. I was researching a script, and I'd heard about her. You know how people are always telling me about weird stuff.''

"Yeah.''

"Not that I believed it, but I thought she'd make a good interview. And—''

"What about Mel and Sebastian?''

"I can't say for sure, but she met him when a client of hers wanted to hire a psychic.'' Nash frowned into his beer. "I know what you're getting at, and you've got a point. Maybe she should have been straight with you earlier.''

He gave a choked laugh. "Maybe?''

"Okay, she should have been. But you don't know the whole story. Morgana told me that Ana was in love with this guy a few years back. She was only about twenty, I think, and really nuts about him. He was an intern at some hospital, and she got the idea that they could work together, that she could help him. So she told him everything and he dumped her. Hard. Apparently he was pretty vicious about it, and with her empathic thing she's really vulnerable to, well... bad vibes, let's say. It left her pretty shaky. She made up her mind she'd go it alone.'' When Boone said nothing, Nash blundered on. "Look, I can't tell you what to do, or how to feel. I just want to say that she wouldn't have done anything to hurt you or Jessie on purpose. She's just not capable of it."

Boone looked toward the house next door. The windows were blank and dark, as they had been for more than a week. "Where is she?"

"She wanted to get away for a little while. Give everybody some room, I guess."

"I haven't seen her since the night she told me. For the first few days, I figured it was better if I stayed away from her." He felt a quick pang of guilt. "I kept Jessie away from her, too. Then, about a week ago, she took off."

"She went to Ireland. She promised to be back before Christmas."

Because his emotions were still raw, Boone only nodded. "I thought I might take Jessie back to Indiana before the holidays. Just for a day or two. Maybe I'll be able to work all this out in my head by the time we all get back."

"Christmas Eve." Padrick sampled the wassail, smacked his lips and sighed. "No better night in the year." Filling a cup, he handed it to his daughter. "Put color in your cheeks, my darling."

"And fire in my blood, the way you make it." But she smiled and sampled. "Isn't it incredible how the twins have grown?"

"Aye." He wasn't fooled by the bright note in her voice. "I can't stand to see my princess so sad."

"I'm not." She squeezed his hand. "I'm fine, Papa. Really."

"I can turn him into a purple jackass for you, darling. I'd be pleasured to."

"No." Because she knew he was only half joking, she kissed his nose. "And you promised we wouldn't have to talk about it once everyone got here."

"Aye, but—"

"A promise," she reminded him, and moved away to help her mother at the stove.

She was glad her house was filled with the people she loved, with the noise of family. There were the scents she had always associated with this holiday. Cinnamon, nutmeg, pine, bayberry. When she'd arrived home a few days before, she'd thrown herself into a flurry of preparations. Tree trimming, present wrapping, cookie baking. Anything and everything to take her mind off the fact that Boone was gone.

That he hadn't spoken to her in more than a month.

But she would survive it. She had already decided what to do, and she refused to let her own unhappiness ruin the family celebration.

"We'll be pleased to have you home with us back in Ireland, Ana." Maureen bent to kiss her daughter's head. "If it's truly what you want."

"I've missed Ireland," Ana said simply. "I think the goose is nearly ready." After opening the oven and taking a heady sniff, she nodded. "Ten minutes more," she predicted. "I'll just go see if everything's on the table."

"Won't even discuss it," Maureen said to her husband when Ana slipped out.

"Tell you what I'd like, my dove. I'd like to take that young man and send him off to some nice frozen island. Just for a day or two, mind."

"If Ana wasn't so sensitive about such matters, I could brew up a nice potion to bring him around."

Padrick patted his wife's bottom. "You have such a delicate touch, Reenie. The lad would be bound by handfast before he could blink—which would be the best thing to happen to him and that darling child of his." He sighed, nibbling his way up his wife's arm. "But Ana would never forgive us for it. We'll have to let her work this out her own way."

Frustrated by a day of canceled flights and delays, Boone slammed the car door. What he wanted was a long hot bath, and what he had to look forward to was an endless night of dealing with those terrifying words *Some Assembly Required.*

If Santa was going to put in an appearance before morning, Boone Sawyer was going to have to put in some overtime.

"Come on, Jess." He rubbed his tired eyes. He'd been traveling for more than twelve hours, if you counted the six he'd spent twiddling his thumbs in the airport. "Let's get this stuff inside."

"Ana's home." Jessie tugged on his arm and pointed toward the lights. "Look, Daddy. There's Morgana's car, and Sebastian's, and the big black car, too. Everybody's at Ana's house."

"I see that." He felt his heart begin to trip a little faster. Then it all but stopped when he saw the For Sale sign in her front yard.

"Can we go over and say merry Christmas? Please, Daddy. I miss Ana." She closed her hand around the zircon she wore. "Can we go say merry Christmas?"

"Yeah." Glaring at the sign, he gripped his daughter's hand. "Yeah, let's go do that. Right now."

Move away, would she? he thought as he strode across the lawn. In a pig's eye. Sell her house when he wasn't looking and just take off? They'd just see about that.

"Daddy, you're walking too fast." Jessie had to trot to keep up. "And you're squeezing my hand."

"Sorry." He drew in a long breath, then let it out again. He scooped her up and took the stairs two at a time. The knock on her door wasn't so much a request as a demand.

It was Padrick who answered, his round face wreathed in a fake white beard, and red stocking cap on his balding head. The minute he saw Boone, the twinkle in his eyes died.

"Well, well, look what the cat dragged in. Brave enough to take us all on at once, are you, boyo? We're not all as polite as my Ana."

"I'd like to see her."

"Oh, would you now? Hold it right there." He gave Jessie his charming smile and lifted her out of Boone's arms. "Looks like I got me a real elf this time. Tell you what, lass, you run right on in and look under that tree. See if there's not something with your name on it."

"Oh, can I?" She hugged Padrick fiercely, then turned back to her father. "Please, can I?"

"Sure." Like Padrick's, his smile faded as soon as Jessie raced inside. "I came to see Ana, Mr. Donovan."

"Well, you're seeing me. What do you think you'd do if someone took your Jessie's heart and squeezed it dry?'' Though he was more than a head shorter than Boone, he advanced, fists raised. ''I won't use nothing but these on you. You've my word as a witch. Now put 'em up.''

Boone didn't know whether to laugh or retreat. ''Mr. Donovan . . .''

''Take the first punch.'' He stuck his whiskered chin out, looking very much like an indignant Santa. ''I'll give you that much, and it's more than you'd be deserving. I've listened to her crying in the night over the likes of you, and it's boiled my blood. Told myself, Padrick, if you get face-to-face with that weasel of a man, you'll have to demolish him. It's a matter of pride.'' He took a swing that spun him completely around and missed Boone by a foot. ''She wouldn't let me go after that other slimy bastard when he broke her poor heart, but I've got you.''

''Mr. Donovan.'' Boone tried again, dodging the peppery blows. ''I don't want to hurt you.''

''Hurt me! Hurt me!'' Padrick was dancing now, fueled by the insult. His Santa cap slipped over his eyes. ''Why, I could turn your insides out. I could give you the head of a badger. I could—''

''Papa!'' With one sharp word, Ana stopped her father's babbling threats.

''You go on inside, princess. This is man's work.''

''I won't have you fighting on my doorstep on Christmas Eve. Now you stop it.''

''Just let me send him to the North Pole. Just for an hour or two. It's only fitting.''

''You'll do no such thing.'' She stepped out and put a warning hand on his shoulder. ''Now go inside and behave, or I'll have Morgana deal with you.''

"Bah! I can handle a witch half my age."

"She's sneaky." Ana pressed a kiss to his cheek. "Please, Papa. Do this for me."

"Could never refuse you anything," he muttered. Then he turned glittering eyes on Boone. "But you watch your step, mister." He jabbed out a plump finger. "You mess with one Donovan, you mess with them all." With a sniff, he went inside.

"I'm sorry," Ana began, fixing a bright smile on her face. "He's very protective."

"So I gathered." Since he wasn't going to have to defend himself after all, he could think of nothing to do with his hands but shove them in his pockets. "I wanted to—we wanted to say merry Christmas."

"Yes, Jessie just did." They were silent for another awkward moment. "You're welcome to come in, have some wassail."

"I don't want to intrude. Your family..." He offered what almost passed for a grin. "I don't want to risk my life, either."

Even the faint smile faded from her eyes. "He wouldn't really have harmed you. It's not our way."

"I didn't mean..." What the hell was he supposed to say to her? "I don't blame him for being upset, and I don't want to make you or your family uncomfortable. If you'd rather, I could just..." He turned slightly, and the sign on her lawn caught his eye. His temper rose accordingly. "What the hell is that?"

"Isn't it clear enough? I'm selling the house. I've decided to go back to Ireland."

"Ireland? You think you can just pack up and move six thousand miles away?"

"Yes, I do. Boone, I'm sorry, but dinner's nearly ready, and I really have to go in. Of course, you're welcome to join us."

"If you don't stop being so bloody polite, I'm going to—" He cut himself off again. "I don't want dinner," he said between his teeth. "I want to talk to you."

"This isn't the time."

"We'll make it the time."

He backed her through the doorway just as Sebastian came down the hall behind her. Placing a light hand on Ana's shoulder, he sent Boone a warning glance. "Is there a problem here, Anastasia?"

"No. I invited Boone and Jessie for dinner, but he isn't able to join us."

"Pity." Sebastian's smile glittered with malice. "Well, then, if you'll excuse us, Sawyer."

Boone slammed the door behind him, causing all the ruckus inside to switch off like a light. Several pairs of eyes turned their way. He was too furious to note that Sebastian's were now bright with amusement.

"Stay out of my way," Boone said quietly. "Each and every one of you. I don't care who you are, or what you are." More than ready to fight a fleet of dragons, he grabbed Ana's hand. "You come with me."

"My family—"

"Can damn well wait." He yanked her back outside.

From her perch under the Christmas tree, Jessie stared wide-eyed after them. "Is Daddy mad at Ana?"

"No." Happy enough about what she'd seen to burst at the seams, Maureen gave the little girl a squeeze. "I think they've just gone off to take care of another Christmas present for you. One I think you'll like best of all."

Outside, Ana labored to keep up. "Stop dragging me, Boone."

"I'm not dragging you," he said as he dragged her through the side yard.

"I don't want to go with you." She felt the tears she'd thought she was finished with stinging her eyes. "I'm not going through this again."

"You think you can put up a stupid sign in your yard and solve everything?" Guided by moonlight, he tugged her down the rock steps that led to the beach. "Drop a bombshell on my head, then take off for Ireland?"

"I can do exactly as I please."

"Witch or no witch, you'd better think that one over again."

"You wouldn't even talk to me."

"I'm talking to you now."

"Well, now I don't want to talk." She broke away and started to climb back up.

"Then you'll listen." He caught her around the waist and tossed her over his shoulder. "And we're going to do this far enough from the house so that I know your family isn't breathing down my neck." When he reached the bottom, he flipped her over and dropped her to her feet. "One step," he warned. "You take one step away and I'll haul you back."

"I wouldn't give you the satisfaction." She struggled with the tears, preferring temper. "You want to have your say. Fine. Then I'll have mine, as well. I accept your position on our relationship. I deeply regret you feel it necessary to keep Jessie away from me."

"I never—"

"Don't deny it. For days before I left for Ireland you kept her at home." She picked up a handful of pebbles and threw them out to sea. "Wouldn't want your little girl too near the witch, after all." She whirled back to him. "For God's sake, Boone, what did you expect from me? Did you see me rubbing my hands together and croaking out, 'I'll get you, my pretty—and your little dog, too'?"

His lips quirked at that, and he reached out, but she spun away. "Give me some credit, Ana."

"I did. A little later than I should have, but I did. And you turned away. Just as I'd known you would."

"Known?" Though he was getting tired of the choreography, he pulled her around again. "How did you know how I'd react? Did you look in your crystal ball, or just have your psychic cousin take a stroll through my head?"

"Neither," she said, with what control she had left. "I wouldn't let Sebastian look, and I didn't look myself, because it seemed unfair. I knew you'd turn away because..."

"Because someone else had."

"It doesn't matter, the fact is you did turn away."

"I just needed to take it in."

"I saw the way you looked at me that night." She shut her eyes. "I've seen that look before. Oh, you weren't cruel like Robert. There were no names, no accusations, but the result was the same. Stay away from me and mine. I don't accept what you are.'' She wrapped her arms tight and cupped her elbows for warmth.

''I'm not going to apologize for having what I think was a very normal reaction. And damn it, Ana, I was tired, and half-crazy. Watching you lie there in bed all those hours, and you were so pale, so still. I was afraid you wouldn't come back. When you did, I didn't know how to treat you. Then you were telling me all of this.''

She searched for calm, knowing it was the best way. ''The timing was bad all around. I wasn't quite strong enough to deal with your feelings.''

''If you had told me before—''

''You would have reacted differently?'' She glanced toward him. ''No, I don't think so. But you're right. I should have. It was unfair, and it was weak of me to let things go as far as they did.''

''Don't put words in my mouth, Ana. Unless you're, what do you call it—linked? If you're not linked with me, you don't know what I'm feeling. It hurt that you didn't trust me.''

She nodded, brushing a tear from her cheek. ''I know. I'm sorry.''

''You were afraid?''

''I told you I was a coward.''

He frowned, watching the hair blow around her face as she stared out at the moon-kissed sea. ''Yes, you did. The night you came across my sketch. The one of the witch. That upset you.''

She shrugged. ''I'm oversensitive sometimes. It was just the mood. I was...''

"About to tell me, and then I scared you off with my evil witch."

"It seemed a difficult time to tell you."

"Because you're a coward," he said mildly, watching her. "Let me ask you something, Ana. What did you do, exactly, to Jessie that day?"

"I linked. I told you I'm an empath."

"It hurt you. I saw." He took her arm, turning her to face him. "Once you cried out, as if it were unbearable. Afterward, you fainted, then slept like the dead for more than a day."

"That's part of it." She tried to push his hand away. It hurt too much to be touched when her defenses were shattered. "When the injuries are so serious, there's a price."

"Yes, I understand. I asked Morgana. She said you could have died. She said the risk was very great because Jessie..." He could hardly say it. "She was gone, or nearly. And you weren't just fixing some broken bones, but bringing her back from the edge. That the line is very fine, and it's very easy for the healer to become the victim."

"What would you have had me do? Let her die?"

"A coward would have. I think your definition and mine are different. Being afraid doesn't make you a coward. You could have saved yourself and let her go."

"I love her."

"So do I. And you gave her back to me. I didn't even thank you."

"Do you think I want your gratitude?" It was too much, she thought. Next he would offer her pity. "I don't. I don't want it. What I did I did freely, because

I couldn't bear to lose her, either. And I couldn't bear for you—''

"For me?'' he said gently.

"For you to lose someone else you loved. I don't want to be thanked for it. It's what I am.''

"You've done it before? What you did with Jessie?''

"I'm a healer. I heal. She was...'' It still hurt to think of it. "She was slipping away. I used what I have to bring her back.''

"It's not that simple.'' His hands were gentle on her arms now, stroking. "Not even for you. You feel more than others. Morgana told me that, too. When you let your defenses down, you're more vulnerable to emotion, to pain, to everything. That's why you don't cry.'' With his fingertip, he lifted a teardrop from her cheek. "But you're crying now.''

"You know everything there is to know. What's the point of this?''

"The point is to take a step back to the night you explained it all to me. The point is for you to take another chance and open yourself up. For me.''

"You ask too much.'' She sobbed the words out, then covered her face. "Oh, leave me alone. Give me some peace. Can't you see how you hurt me?''

"Yes, I can see.'' He wrapped his arms around her, fighting to soothe while she struggled for release. "You've lost weight, you're pale. When I look into your eyes, I see every ounce of pain I caused you. I don't know how to take it back. I don't know how your father kept himself from cursing me with whatever was in his arsenal.''

"We can't use power to harm. It's against everything we are. Please let me go."

"I can't. I almost thought I could. She lied to me, I told myself. She betrayed my trust. She isn't real." He kept a firm grip on her arms as he pulled her away. "It doesn't matter. None of it matters. If it's magic, I don't want to lose it. I can't lose you. I love you, Ana. All that you are. Please." He touched his lips to hers, tasting tears. "Please come back to me."

The shaft of hope was almost painful. She clung to it, to him. "I want to believe."

"So do I." He cupped her face, kissing her again. "And I do. I believe in you. In us. If this is my fairy tale, I want to play it out."

She stared up at him. "You can accept all of this? All of us?"

"I figure I'm pretty well suited to do just that. Of course, it might take a while for me to convince your father not to do something drastic to my anatomy." He traced his fingers over her lips as they curved. "I didn't know if you'd ever smile for me again. Tell me you still love me. Give me that, too."

"Yes, I love you." Her lips trembled under his. "Always."

"I won't hurt you again." He brushed away tears with his thumbs. "I'll make up for everything."

"It's done." She caught his hands. "That's done. We have tomorrow."

"Don't cry anymore."

She smiled, rubbing her fists across her cheeks. "No, I won't. I never cry."

He took those damp fists and kissed them. "You said to ask you again. It's been longer than a week, but

I'm hoping you haven't forgotten what you said your answer would be."

"I haven't forgotten."

"Put your hand here." He pressed her palm to his heart. "I want you to feel what I feel." He linked his free hand with hers. "The moon's almost full. The first time I kissed you was in the moonlight. I was charmed, enchanted, spellbound. I always will be. I need you, Ana."

She could feel the strength of that love pouring into her. "You have me."

"I want you to marry me. Share the child you gave back to me. She's yours as much as mine now. Let me make more children with you. I'll take you as you are, Anastasia. I swear I'll cherish you as long as I live."

She lifted her arms to him. Hair like sunlight. Eyes like smoke. Shafts of moonglow shimmered around her like torchlight.

"I've been waiting for you."

Epilogue

Alone on a wild crag facing a stormy sea stood Donovan Castle. This dark night, lightning flashed and shuddered in the black sky, and the wind set the leaded glass to shaking in the diamond panes.

Inside, fires leaped and glowed in the hearths. Those who were witches, and those who were not, gathered close, waiting for the indignant wail that would signal a new life.

"Are you cheating, Grandda?" Jessie asked Padrick as he perused his cards.

"Cheating!" He gave a merry laugh and wiggled his brows. "Certainly I am. Go fish."

She giggled and drew from the pile. "Granny Maureen says you always cheat." She tilted her head. "Were you really a frog?"

"That I was, darling. A fine green one."

She accepted this, just as she accepted the other wonders of her life with the Donovans. She petted the snoring Daisy, who rested her big golden head in Jessie's lap. "Will you be a frog again sometime, so I can see?"

"I might surprise you." He winked and changed her hand of cards into a rainbow of lollipops.

"Oh, Grandda," she said indulgently.

"Sebastian?" Mel hustled down the main stairs and shouted into the parlor, where her husband was sipping brandy and watching the card game. "Shawn and Keely are awake and fussing. I have my hands full helping with Ana."

"Be right there." The proud papa of three months set down his snifter and headed up to change diapers.

Nash bounced one-year-old Allysia on his knee while Donovan sat in Matthew's lap playing with his pocket watch. "Be careful he doesn't eat it," Nash commented. "Or make it disappear. We're having a little trouble keeping him in line."

"The lad needs to spread his wings a bit."

"If you say so. But when I went to get him out of his crib the other day, it was full of rabbits. Real ones."

"Takes after his mother," Matthew said proudly. "She ran us ragged."

Allysia leaned back against her father and smiled. Instantly Daisy woke and trotted over. Within seconds, every dog and cat in the house was swarming through the room.

"Ally," Nash said with a sigh. "Remember how we said one at a time?"

"Doggies." Squealing, Ally tugged gently on the ears of Matthew's big silver wolf. "Kittycats."

"Next time just one, okay?" Nash plucked a cat off his shoulder, nudged another off the arm of the chair. "A couple of weeks ago she had every hound within ten miles howling in the yard. Come on, monsters." He rose, tucking Allysia, then Donovan, under his arms like footballs. They kicked and giggled. "I think it's time for bed."

"Story," Donovan demanded. "Uncle Boone."

"He's busy. You'll have to settle for one from your old man."

He was indeed busy, watching a miracle. The room was scented with candles and herbs, warmed by the fire glowing in the hearth. He held tight to Ana as she brought their son into the world.

Then their daughter.

Then their second son.

"Three." He kept saying it over and over, even as Bryna settled an infant in his arms. "Three." They'd told him there would be triplets, but he hadn't really believed it.

"Runs in the family." Exhausted, elated, Ana took another bundle from Morgana. She pressed her lips gently to the silky cheek. "Now we have two of each."

He grinned down at his wife as Mel settled the third baby in the crook of Ana's arm. "I think we need a bigger house."

"We'll add on."

"Would you like the others to come up?" Bryna asked gently. "Or would you rather rest awhile?"

"No, please." Ana tilted her head so that it rested against Boone's arm. "Ask them to come up."

They crowded in, making too much noise. Ana made room in the big bed for Jessie to sit beside her, then placed a baby in her arms.

"This is your brother, Trevor. Your sister, Mauve. And your other brother, Kyle."

"I'm going to take good care of them. Always. Look, Grandda, we have a big family now."

"You do indeed, my little lamb." He blew heartily into his checked kerchief. He wiped his runny eyes and looked mistily at Boone. "Just as well I didn't flatten you when I had the chance."

"Here." Boone held out a squealing infant. "Hold your grandson."

"Ah, Maureen, my cheesecake, look at this. He has my eyes."

"No, my frog prince, he has mine."

They argued, with the rest of the Donovans throwing their weight to one side or the other. Boone slipped his arm around his wife, held his family close as his son suckled greedily at his first taste of mother's milk. Lightning flashed against the windows, the wind howled, and the fire leapt high in the grate.

Somewhere deep in the forest, high in the hills, the faeries danced.

And they lived happily ever after.

* * * * *

COMING NEXT MONTH

CHERISH
Sherryl Woods

Read the third book in the *Vows* series.

World War II had abruptly come between Brandon
Halloran and the girl of his dreams, Elizabeth
Forsythe. Could the love of a lifetime be rekindled
so many years later?

IT MUST HAVE BEEN THE MISTLETOE
Nikki Benjamin

The link between Dominic Fabrino and Martha
Townsend was her old banger. She'd asked
Dominic to fix her car, but he was more interested
in her heart. Perhaps the Christmas mistletoe would
be useful?

A PRINCE AMONG MEN
Mona van Wieren

Trevor Lloyd had found the woman who haunted
his dreams. But his ideal woman claimed that he
didn't fit in her plans—as if she thought that would
stop him. As if destiny could be sidetracked. . .

Silhouette Special Edition

COMING NEXT MONTH

WHEN SOMEBODY NEEDS YOU
Trisha Alexander

Journalist Jack Forrester thought Desiree Cantrelle
was the key to a dark mystery that had brought him to
New Orleans. So he followed her deep into
Louisiana's bayou country—deep into the past . . .

JEZEBEL'S BLUES
Ruth Winds

When dark and unpredictable Eric Putman appeared
on her doorstep, seeking shelter from the weather,
Celia Moon was tempted to deny him entry but she
put aside her common sense. . . and she let him in. . .

GYPSY SUMMER
Patricia Coughlin

Jennifer McVeigh had taken her sons back to her
home town. She was seeking safety and stability—
two words she'd never associated with the town's
notorious bad boy Rex Lovell. Was she just a passing
fancy for Rex?

Another Face . . .
Another Identity . . .
Another Chance . . .

When her teenage love turns to hate, Geraldine Frances vows to even the score. After arranging her own "death", she embarks on a dramatic transformation emerging as *Silver*, a hauntingly beautiful and mysterious woman few men would be able to resist.

With a new face and a new identity, she is now ready to destroy the man responsible for her tragic past.

Silver – a life ruled by one all-consuming passion, is Penny Jordan at her very best.

W●RLDWIDE

An irresistible offer from Silhouette

Here's a personal invitation for you to become a regular reader of Special Editions. And we'd like to welcome you with 4 books, a cuddly teddy bear and a special mystery gift - all absolutely FREE and with no obligation whatsoever!

Then, each month you could look forward to receiving 6 Special Editions delivered to your door, postage and packing FREE! Plus our Newsletter FREE, featuring authors, competitions, special offers and lots more...

It's so easy. Send no money now but simply complete the coupon below and return it today to: **Silhouette Reader Service, FREEPOST, PO Box 236, Croydon, Surrey CR9 9EL.**

✂

YES Please rush me 4 FREE Silhouette Special Editions and 2 FREE gifts! Please also reserve me a Reader Service subscription, which mea I can look forward to receiving 6 brand new Special Editions for only £11.10 each month. Postage and packing is FREE and so is my monthly Newsletter. If I choose not to subscribe, I shall write to you within 10 da and still keep the FREE books and gifts. I may cancel or suspend my subscription at any time simply by writing to you. I am over 18 years of age.   Please write in BLOCK CAPITA

Ms/Mrs/Miss/Mr _____ EP43

Address _____

_____

_____ Postcode _____

Signature _____

Offer closes 31st October 1993. The right is reserved to refuse an application and change the terms of this offer. One application per household. Overseas readers please write for details. Southern Africa write to Book Services International Ltd., Box 41654, Craighall, Transvaal 2024. You may be mailed with offers from other reputable companies as a result of this application. Please tick box if you would prefer not to receive such offers ☐